A Thompson Sisters Novella

Falling Stars

BOOKS BY CHARLES SHEEHAN-MILES

Thompson Sisters
A Song for Julia
Falling Stars
Just Remember to Breathe
The Last Hour
Rachel's Peril (coming December 2013)

America's Future
Republic
Insurgent

Prayer at Rumayla
A Novel of the Gulf War

Saving the World on Thirty Dollars a Day: An Activist's Guide
to Starting, Organizing and Running a Non-Profit Organization

A Thompson Sisters Novella

Falling Stars

Charles Sheehan-Miles

Cincinnatus Press

If you enjoyed this book, please share it with a friend, write a review online, or send feedback to the author!

www.sheehanmiles.com

Published by Cincinnatus Press
United States of America

ISBN-13: 978-0-9898688-5-3

Printed in the United States of America
Cincinnatus Press
www.cincinnatuspress.com

v11282013

CHAPTER ONE

She Hates Me

Your personal effects (Crank)

"Your personal effects."

The red-faced, surly, rounded cop behind the desk slid a thick brown envelope across to me. I opened it. Inside I found my wallet and the belt loop chain it attached to, along with my belt and shoelaces. The room had the hard reality of a hangover. I'd been through this routine once...or twice...before.

"Thanks," I mumbled.

The cranky cop gave me a sardonic grin. "Have a nice day."

I snorted and rolled my eyes. The other cop pointed to the door; I heard a buzz then pushed my way out, my laceless boots flopping around my feet with every step.

Julia stood up when she saw me, her long auburn hair falling in loose ringlets around her shoulders, her blue-green eyes fixing on mine. In this setting, the lobby of a urine-smelling jail, she looked out of place, a flower in a field of manure. But appearances can be deceiving.

"Are you okay?" She raised her right hand to tentatively touch my cheek. "You've got a black eye."

"Yeah, it's fine, babe."

At that, her eyes narrowed and the hand tenderly touching my cheek slapped me hard on the shoulder.

"Ow!"

"What is *wrong* with you?" she asked.

"What the hell did I do?"

"Just come on, we've got to pick up Sean and Carrie."

She turned and marched out the front door of the jail. Not a kiss or an, "I'm glad you're okay," or anything. What the hell? Sometimes I didn't understand her. I loved her. She was my life, but... Christ, this summer had been frustrating as hell.

My car was parked across the street. A mint, cherry-red 1968 Ford Mustang convertible with a white racing stripe and a silver skull in place of the Mustang logo on the front. I'd gotten a deal on the car in LA, provoking one of many arguments with Julia while we were on tour. What the hell did she care if I bought a car? Especially a car that rocked? But no...apparently *my* buying a car warranted fourteen days of discussion.

I felt around in my pockets for my keys, but of course I didn't have them, and then she was unlocking the driver's side *and getting in* while I stood there, a cold wind from the bay biting through my thin t-shirt.

"Wait... I'll drive," I protested.

She gave me a wry look. "Are you sober enough to drive yet?"

I brought my eyebrows together and thought about it. I felt sober enough. But... It wasn't worth the fight. "Fine, you drive."

I got in the passenger side and slumped into my seat. She cranked the car, then hit play on the stereo. Puddle of Mud's *She Hates Me* blasted out of the speakers. I winced. I loved loud music, but for fuck's sake, it was six in the morning and my head hurt.

She put the car in gear. I stared out the window. It was getting light outside, and soon it would be Saturday morning in San Francisco. I loved what little I'd seen of the city since we arrived yesterday morning, but part of the frustration of traveling on tour was a tight schedule. One city started to look like the next, one hotel like the next, one argument like the next. It had all run together, colorless.

"How's Sean?" I asked.

She gave me a sour look. "How do you think he is, Crank? He's stressed and upset and worried about you."

"Well, it's not like I went out and intentionally got arrested, Julia."

"No, you just beat someone up *right in front of the cops.*"

"He was a prick."

"No, he was a member of the media."

"Same thing."

She shook her head. "Stop acting like a child, Crank. There's a hundred bands out there wanting to be where you are. You want to kill your career right out the door, keep this attitude up and keep pissing off the press. Let's go get your brother before he has a complete meltdown."

"Fine."

I winced as she took a corner too fast, and then she was driving along the waterfront toward our hotel. I could see glimpses of the water through the buildings, tourists, and tourist traps. I kept my eyes out there, trying to relax just a little.

Okay, look. I get it. She was right. I could've kept my cool. I *should've* kept my cool. But lately it seemed like we couldn't go anywhere or do anything without having reporters shoving their cameras in our faces. We were going through a pack of them, and lights were flashing, they were shoving at us, and I could hear the tone in Sean's voice as he started to lose it. So I lost it for him. Shoot me already.

Basically, the bad news was, everywhere we went, we had reporters and paparazzi dogging us. And the good news was, everywhere we went, we had reporters and paparazzi dogging us. Seriously. That doesn't happen unless you're a success. And increasingly, my band, Morbid Obesity, was just that.

Being perfectly modest, it was because the music freaking rocked, but also because we had an amazing, talented manager in the form of my girlfriend, Julia. Julia, who helped find every opportunity for our band to be successful. Julia, who had become almost a big sister for my brother, Sean. Julia, who I absolutely loved.

Julia, who lately wasn't happy with me at all.

Could I blame her? It's not like I hadn't been a complete dick over and over again. But then again, she was no saint either.

Whatever. We had a nice, five day drive ahead of us, all the way across the country. A chance for us to relax and calm down. A chance for us to remind each other why we loved each other. To leave behind the stress and distractions of the tour.

A chance to be *us* again.

Botulism? (Crank)

When Julia got me out of jail, my head was splitting. By the time we picked up Sean at the hotel and were on the road to the Richmond neighborhood of San Francisco, it was nearly noon and the pain in my head had progressed to excruciating. I needed a drink and then some lunch, in that order.

On second thought, I was so queasy, maybe I'd skip the lunch. Julia had insisted I get a shower before we head to her parents', which was probably best considering the opinion they already held of me, and all that steam and hot water left me more dehydrated. A drink it is.

I shifted in my seat, looking back at Sean. He had a book in his lap, a worn out 1990s edition of *Off the Beaten Path*, a travel guide to the obscure and weird all across the United States. He'd been asking for days about several sights he wanted to see along our route.

"You doing okay, Sean?"

"I'm well. Are you? I'm concerned about infection around your right eye. Or other complications. Have you had any changes or loss of vision?"

Jesus, Sean. I nodded slowly. "Yeah, a little. Why?"

Sean's forehead creased. "Can you move your eyes?"

I wanted to growl at him. Instead, I looked to the left, then the right.

"No, no," he said, "hold your head still. Look only with your eyes."

I did, and it hurt. *A lot.* "All right, so what if it hurts?"

He leaned forward and grabbed the side of my head. I jerked back.

"Crank, please stay in one place," he ordered calmly.

I rolled my eyes, but stayed still. I was nothing if not a quick learner.

He leaned close, looking in my eyes. "Your eyes aren't leaking any fluids. If you notice any, we need to call an ambulance immediately.

"I'm not going blind, am I?" I was embarrassed I'd asked the question. Suddenly I was wishing I hadn't hit that reporter. I was too young to go blind or get some kind of brain infection. Maybe I needed to go to the doctor now.

Julia just kept driving. We were going uphill now, way uphill. We passed street signs for Clement and Geary, Anza, then Balboa. At least I could still read—that was a good sign, right?

I turned back to Sean. "Are you sure I shouldn't go to the doctor now?"

"Relax, Crank," Julia said.

"There are really no guarantees," Sean said. "A black eye is probably the only complication. There's a minor chance of more serious side effects, though."

"What kind of side effects?"

Julia turned onto Cabrillo Street, shaking her head slightly as she did so. She had a wry smile on her face.

"Nothing really to worry about unless you have a severe headache."

Problem was, I *did* have a severe headache. Of course I had a headache, I'd drunk a lot at the party and been punched in the face. But maybe Sean was right. What if something more serious was wrong? "What if I do, though?"

"Well, obviously eye leakage would be pretty bad. And in some cases the eye's been known to fill up with fluid or blood. That would be bad. But it's not the worst case."

"Well, what the hell is?"

"Oh, well that would be a cerebral hemorrhage."

I shook my head, but the fifty punk rockers dancing in my skull took issue with that. "What is that? Speak English, Sean."

"That's an intracranial hemorrhage, but what makes it special is that it bleeds directly into the brain tissue itself."

"Special?" I cried. "It's special? Oh, for God's sake, Sean, knock it *off*. If I'm going to die, at least I can die ignorant."

Julia burst into laughter. "You're not going to die, Crank. You need a drink of water and some aspirin."

"Fine. Stop at the drugstore, then?"

"We're here," she said.

Here was a block of four and five-story row houses. She expertly parallel parked in front of one of them, an imposing four story-edifice of blue brick and ornate stonework. At ground level was a garage door directly next to a small stoop and a front door.

Julia sat rigidly in her seat, both hands gripping the steering wheel.

"What's wrong?"

Her eyes darted to the house, then to me, and it sank in. I knew exactly what was wrong.

"Hey," I said quietly. "I'll behave."

She closed her eyes, and for a second it seemed she was trying to not cry. Then she said, her voice at a near whisper, "Come on."

I reached out and touched her arm. "Julia?"

She took her hands off the wheel and shook them in the air as if warding off insects, then opened the door and stepped out of the car.

I looked over my shoulder at Sean. He shrugged, then said at his usual near shout, "She seems upset, Crank."

I shook my head. "Thanks for the insight."

Something was just off. I mean, Julia and I have had fights. Occasionally we've even had some really rough ones. And the way it went was pretty predictable—big blowout, followed by equally big make up. And the makeup sex was usually hot, which is a plus.

What Julia usually wasn't was sullen. Quiet. Withdrawn. Not since the first few months I'd known her, when her walls were still coming down. To be completely honest? It was starting to piss me off. Yeah, I screwed up and spent the night in jail. But maybe be understanding for a change?

She was my girlfriend, for Christ's sake! She was the woman I loved. Why the hell not behave like it?

Christ on a sidecar. Sean and I followed her through the front door of the house. I was behind her, but close enough to her side to see it when she slid her smile back on like a mask.

She opened the door, but reached out and pressed the doorbell, then called out, "Hello!"

It seemed odd... No matter how long I'd lived away from home, I still just walked in. But Julia's family wasn't like mine. Not at all. Back home, Dad would be puttering around the kitchen, ready to crack a joke or pass a beer to anyone who dropped by. Not retired Ambassador Thompson or his witch of a wife, Adelina. From what Julia had told me, she'd never really lived in this house, just visited during the holidays, because the whole Thompson clan moved here when her dad retired just a couple years ago—after Julia had already left home for college.

At Julia's shout, a stampede of small feet came down the stairs: four little girls. Alexandra, the eldest of the four, was thirteen now. She had golden brown hair framing pretty green eyes and looked substantially older than she had just a year ago. She was going be a knockout, and I felt an instinctive protectiveness. There was a whole world of complete dicks out there; guys like me, when I was her age, who were nothing but trouble. I wanted to shield her from it.

Alexandra hugged Julia, but the twins headed straight for me, with Sarah leading the charge. "Crank!" she shouted, launching herself from the fourth step up straight at me. Luckily I caught her before she broke my neck, and next thing I knew both twins were hugging me and grabbing at my leather jacket. Weird, because I'd only met them twice. I guess I made a good impression.

Andrea, the youngest, stayed back. She was six now and already taller than her seven-year-old twin sisters. She looked like a tiny version of Carrie, the second eldest of the six sisters. Carrie was six-two and when she walked into a room curtains smoldered and windows blew open. To be honest, she intimidated the fuck out of me. Julia was beautiful.

Incredibly so. But all of us paled beside Carrie, a graceful creature who seemed to come from another planet.

I followed Julia and Alexandra up the stairs with one twin on each hip. It was a good thing I'd been eating my Wheaties. Well, I hadn't, actually, so when I got to the top of the stairs, I found myself wishing first, that I had a cigarette, second, that I'd never smoked a cigarette in my life, and third, that I knew where the restroom was so I could go vomit in peace. Instead, I found myself easing the twins to the floor and shaking hands with Richard Thompson.

He wore brown corduroy pants and a tweed jacket. Seriously. This guy was right out of the 1970s and looked kind of like Mister Rogers. Except for his cold eyes. Something about him just freaked me out. Even when he smiled and was friendly, which was pretty much always, it never really reached his eyes. He was strangely unlike his wife, who was caustic and mean to her daughters, but at least you knew where you stood.

"Crank," he said, "you look well." His hands were dry and his grip firm; he looked me dead in the eye as he said the words, one eyebrow slightly raised.

I felt off balance. Even I knew I looked like shit right now. Why the lie? I blinked my eyes and pictured Julia's father strapped to a revolving circus target thingy in a clown suit while the twins threw water balloons filled with paint at him. That vision made me smile. A lot. I returned his handshake with enthusiasm. "Yeah, I'm doing great, Ambassador Thompson, how about you? Retirement's suiting you?"

He nodded. "Quite. I'm writing my memoirs."

"You must have a lot to write about, with all that travel, huh?"

"You have no idea," he responded.

"This is my brother, Sean."

Mr. Thompson stuck his hand out to shake. This was always a delicate moment with Sean. Shaking hands is one of those customs which makes little sense to him—we'd talked about it before. "I don't understand why it's ever necessary," he always said. Then he'd mount his objections. Touching hands with people, especially strangers, was unhygienic. Sean once spent two full days telling me all the various infections, bacteria, viruses and fungi which can be spread via handshake. All I could think at the time was, if just *shaking hands* could do that, what all could you get from sleeping with someone? It was three weeks before I could touch a girl after that.

So as Sean shook Mr. Thompson's hand, all I could think was *botulism?* But Sean wasn't interested in talking about infections right now. Because no sooner did they shake hands than he said, "Want to know something ironic? I read that in the 1980s, there were a lot of very shady dealings with the Mujahideen in Afghanistan that led to the formation of the Taliban, and that the United States funded a lot of that. Isn't it odd that the United States would arm and fund the very people who came back and attacked us?"

I'll admit my eyes widened, and I saw Julia startle too. Sean had never talked about anything political in front of us before. Now he was off like a storm, asking Mr. Thompson if he knew the details of the financial dealings between the anti-Soviet rebels of the 1980s, the Central Intelligence Agency, and the State Department.

Mr. Thompson was pale. "I really can't talk about any of that sort of thing," he said. "I'm sure you know it's classified."

"But *why* is it classified? That was a long time ago. And it's in the public's best interest to know," Sean asked at almost the level of a shout, because that's just the way he talked.

I'm pretty sure poor Mr. Thompson, who never spoke above a low, cultured tone, had no idea how to handle this loud, monotone, strange teenager.

"Come on, Sean," I said, because it was clear Mr. Thompson was finished with this discussion.

Mr. Thompson stepped back, not even attempting to hide his annoyance, but his words were as smooth as a raspberry lime rickey. "I hope you'll forgive me if I can't join you all for lunch. I've got an important phone call coming in."

I'd been intimidated by Richard Thompson before. I'd been annoyed by his snobbish attitude, his disapproval. I'd been made to feel small by the way he looked down his nose at me. But I'd never felt blind rage. Not until now. Because when he said those words, Julia shrank just a little, her shoulders falling even as she gave him a counterfeit smile and responded, "No problem, Dad, I know you're busy."

The old bastard slinked back into his office and we were enveloped in chaos again as Carrie stumbled to the main floor and bumped into her mother, who was just walking in from the kitchen.

"Carrie," Mrs. Thompson scolded, "watch where you're going!"

Carrie straightened, but I could tell it was an effort. By all appearances, she was as hungover as I was—hair a mess, eyes bleary, skin pale. Last night at the after party, she'd done more drinking than was a good idea for any seventeen-year-old. Apparently she regretted it this morning.

Mrs. Thompson turned to Julia only after she'd chastened her next eldest daughter. She spoke in a breezy, almost friendly tone. "Julia, I'm so happy to see you. I've been at my wits' end with worry this summer. You must tell me everything."

Okay, that was just weird. Really weird. Julia has nightmares about her mother and here she was being super friendly.

Whatever. I followed them into the dining room, preceded by Andrea and Alexandra and flanked by the twins, my own little honor guard. Carrie was just putting a plate on the dining table when we walked in. It was already set with plates adorned by dainty little sandwiches cut into triangles. I eyeballed the sandwiches. Turkey and Swiss? I thought about my stomach for a second, trying to decide if I'd be able to manage eating, and decided that yes, I would.

When we walked in, Carrie's eyes went to Sean. They'd met, briefly, at the after party the night before. *Just before I got arrested.* Now, Carrie saw Sean, then looked away, her cheeks going a little red.

That was odd. Had he said something obnoxious to her? Because it couldn't be...

Now that I thought about it, I took a good look at my brother. He was Carrie's height, two inches over six feet, and had spent a lot of the last nine months working out. At first I'd thought it was weird, until I realized his workout regimen was designed to deter the bullies at his high school. He'd developed powerful muscles in his chest and arms; I wouldn't want to tangle with him. His hair, cropped short, framed blue eyes. He looked... not like I thought of him. He looked like a young man. Sean was my little brother. When I looked at him, I saw meltdowns. I saw struggles with basic interactions with other people. I saw the boy who wept after the assholes at his school stuffed his favorite hat down the toilet.

Apparently Carrie saw something else.

Andrea held back when we came in the room, but the twins ran for the table. Jessica, who had the same brown hair and green eyes as Alex, stopped at a sharp word from her mother. But Sarah...black hair, light blue eyes, all expressive attitude, climbed right up into her chair and grabbed a sandwich.

At the sight of Sarah suddenly gobbling forbidden food, Andrea and Jessica froze. Carrie's eyes darted back and forth between Sarah and her mother, and Julia just shook her head.

"Young lady!" Mrs. Thompson shouted loud enough to shatter windows.

Sean lifted his hands to his ears as if to block out the sound, and Sarah shouted back, "Hungry!" and stuffed the sandwich into her mouth.

Let me tell you something. Back in the day I used to go with Wheezy and Gearhead and Lenny and hang out in the cemetery and get wasted, and sometimes we'd get high on whatever we could afford. It was all fun and games, and when the cops came around we'd run like hell through the gravestones and out into the neighborhood, cutting between houses and gardens to get away. Half the fun was outwitting the cops. But anyway, that's not the point. The point is, one time I was running through the gravestones and it had rained the night before, so the ground was slick. I felt my feet slip out from under me and I went sliding along, then slammed into a wall. It knocked the air out of me, which was no big deal, and almost got me caught, which was. But then I heard the cop behind me slide, and he didn't make a nice soft thump like I did. He hit something with a loud crack and cried out.

Aw, shit, I thought. See, maybe I was trouble, but my dad was a cop. And that guy was probably somebody's dad. Suddenly it had stopped being a game. I ducked my head around the gravestone, and there he was.

A Cambridge cop, and worse, one I knew. Officer Brandon McCaffrey. Yeah, I knew him. He knew my dad. It was all one big incestuous family. And from the look on his face, Officer McCaffrey was in a world of pain.

I couldn't leave him. So I slid back around the gravestone and said, "Shit. Let me call for help."

Bad idea. See, I didn't think. Officer McCaffrey had a radio and was perfectly capable of calling for help. He had a nightstick too, and he was pretty good at using it. From a supine position in incredible pain from a broken ankle, he still managed to clip me right on the temple with said nightstick, knocking me out. McCaffrey spent the rest of the winter working behind a desk. I spent two nights in the hospital and two weeks in jail.

And the icy, murderous expression on his face right before he knocked me cold? That was the expression Adelina Thompson had on her face when she started walking toward Sarah, who had at that point consumed the entire triangle of sandwich.

You can't really blame her. Sarah was being intentionally defiant. And then it got worse. Because when Adelina started for her, Sarah jumped onto the table and ran for dear life. Her little feet knocked over a plate with a sandwich, then a pitcher of milk—seriously, who puts milk in a pitcher?—and then they were moving faster than her body and she started to slide on the table in the spilled milk, straight toward Carrie, whose eyes had widened.

"Young lady!" Adelina screamed.

Sean, who had thus far only managed to mortally offend one of Julia's parents, decided it was time to start on the other one. With a full-throated roar, he shouted, *"Let's all start screaming!"*

Jessica and Andrea both burst into tears, and an astonished Adelina forgot all about Sarah, who made her getaway by sliding down the length of the table until she slammed into Carrie at the end. Carrie swung her to the floor and Sarah ran out the door. Adelina stared at Sean, slack-jawed, and I said, "Sean, stop!"

Julia raced to Sean and she did something I'd never seen anyone but our mother do successfully. She put her hands on both of his shoulders and looked him eye to eye as best she could, given that he was nearly a foot taller than her. "Sean. Calm. Down." Her voice was firm, calm, and loving; hearing it brought tears to my eyes, because lately all I'd heard from her were the strained voices of stress, anger and sadness.

Sean took a breath and closed his eyes. Silence fell.

Talk to me (Julia)

I surveyed the chaos of Sarah's departure for about five seconds. A mixture of milk and mustard was smeared from the center of the dinner table down to the end, an impressionist painting by an eccentric artist with primary colors and a brush made of Keds. The pattern continued on the floor and right out the door of the dining room.

Sean had taken a deep breath and stopped shouting. My mother, however, was just about to get started again, and she didn't know that anything she did now would just make things worse. Crank looked hungover and irritable, so he wasn't going to help solve anything.

"Mother, I think we should just skip lunch at this point. I'll go up and help Carrie finish packing. Sean and Crank, do you think you can get the car ready for Carrie's stuff?"

I raised my eyebrows as I looked at Crank, hoping against hope he'd catch my drift. It wouldn't take the two of them any time at all, but that wasn't the point. The point was to separate my mother and Sean before one of them said something unforgivable.

Crank nodded and I breathed a sigh of relief. "Come on, Sean," he said, and the two of them headed back down the stairs.

My mother looked at me, alarm on her face. "Julia, what—"

I held a palm up. "Mother...just... Stop. Don't ask."

Her eyes narrowed and she opened her mouth to say something which would undoubtedly be awful.

"*Please*, Mother. It's fine. Let me help clean up in here, okay?"

She gave me a dismissive look. "No. You go with Carrie. Everyone... out!"

I didn't need to hear that twice. I left right on Carrie's heels, both of us light years behind the younger girls, who had managed to vanish without a trace. And that was no wonder, really. I tried to run away from our mother any chance I could.

I hadn't been in Carrie's room since Christmas, but it looked much the same. A huge black poster showed a green planet, apparently sticking its tongue out, if planets could have tongues, with the reminder "DON'T PANIC" printed in large, friendly letters. Her bookshelves were doubled and tripled up, books stacked sideways and in crazy directions. The desk was clear; a close inspection would turn up certain items and keepsakes missing. Her closet, hanging open, was nearly empty. She was obviously ready to leave.

She only had two suitcases, but one of them was very large.

"I just need to get a couple last things in here," she said.

"Take your time," I murmured. I leaned against the window, looking to Cabrillo Street below. Crank and Sean had the trunk of the Mustang open and were pulling things out. I glanced at the trunk, then Carrie's suitcases. We should be okay.

"What's going on with you and Crank?" she asked.

"What?"

She tugged on the zipper to one of her suitcases, trying her hardest to get it closed. It was resisting her. I walked over and held the suitcase still.

"Don't try to snow me, Julia."

I shrugged. "We've... It..." I closed my eyes because I didn't know how to say it.

She stopped with the suitcase. "Julia? Talk to me."

I shook my head. "We've just... It's been awful. The tour." To my horror, I felt my throat closing. Tears, unwanted, unwarranted, out of control, were clawing their way out. I forced them back.

"What's been awful?" she asked.

I didn't know where to begin. It had started with a stupid argument really. Crank had gotten pissed one day when he saw me talking with Preston Reeve. I found myself shaking my head. "I'll... It's complicated. Really complicated. I'll tell you later, okay? Right now let's just get going."

She nodded her head. "All right. But we're talking before this is all over, okay?"

We got her suitcases closed and headed downstairs to say our good-byes and load up the car. I'd managed to avoid voicing the one thing I truly didn't want to say, the thing that would ruin our trip and break my heart, which was I didn't think I could stay with Crank anymore and that this trip was going to be our goodbye.

CHAPTER TWO

Head-on Collision

I can't hear you (Julia)

"re you insane?"

I wouldn't have asked the question, but Crank had taken a left turn going the wrong way down a one-way street, prompting horns from the wall of cars rushing at us down the extremely steep hill and screams from the back seat. The screams didn't stop as Crank shouted, "Oh, fuck me!" and put the car into reverse, backing partly onto Geary Boulevard and partly onto the sidewalk. We did, however, come to an instant stop when he hit a telephone pole with the rear bumper.

Crank took a slow breath, then looked over at me. "Sorry."

"Are you sober? Enough to make this drive?" My heart was thumping. I knew my tone was harsh. I sounded like my mother.

I'd never been so scared in my life.

"Yeah, I just... This city... Christ..."

Carrie, sitting behind Crank, leaned forward and put a hand on his shoulder. "It's okay... it's a confusing city. If you go straight here, then take a right on Van Ness, that'll get us there, okay?"

He nodded. "Yeah. I've got this. Thanks."

Sean, behind me, said, "I'm not so sure. The residual effects of alcohol can last for days in some circumstances, and Crank isn't that stable to begin with."

"Knock it off, Sean!" Crank's voice was strained, but he also sounded so much like his dad, Jack, that I almost did a double take. Irritation on his face, he put the car in drive and pulled back into traffic, this time going in the correct direction.

I leaned my elbow on the window frame, trying not to look. Trying not to think. Too much thinking took me right back down into the swirling disaster this entire summer has been, so I stared out the window as Crank drove us up I-80 and the Bay Bridge. It was easier not to fight about it anymore. It was easier to not think about it, especially to not think about how afraid I was. Afraid I was going to lose him. Afraid I wasn't.

All I had to do was close my eyes and think about the after party in Dallas to see disaster after disaster. Crank's sudden, inexplicable jealousy. How the groupies screamed his name. The pained, sad expression on his face and how he turned away from me. All I had to do was close my eyes to see his hand on that blonde girl's ass.

Holding back tears, I stared off to the side. The girders of the Bay Bridge passed us by, waves and whitecaps far below. To the south, over the bay, I could see clouds in the distance, dark clouds. They looked like rain and I hoped we weren't headed into a storm. I'd had enough storms this year.

I glanced back over my shoulder. Sean was leaning back in his seat, staring up at the upper level of the bridge above us. He had a nervous expression on his face. His arms were crossed over his chest, and he was squeezed as far away from Carrie as he could possibly get and still remain inside the vehicle. He'd gotten really upset last night when the photographers ambushed us on the way out of the party; upset enough that Crank lost it and punched the photographer and got himself arrested.

Sean and Carrie had seemed to hit it off at the party, but now he looked like he was trying to crawl out of the car to get away from her. For her part, she was looking out over the opposite side of the bridge, arms crossed over her chest, a frown on her face. Her hair was blowing all over the place.

"Carrie?" I called.

She looked over at me, an expression of annoyance on her face. "You okay?" I asked.

In a jerky motion, she widened her eyes and crossed them, shrugged her shoulders and threw her arms out to the side as if she were saying, "What the hell is wrong with you?"

"What?" I asked.

She tapped her ears, then leaned close. "I can't hear you!" she shouted. "It's loud back here with the top down!"

She leaned close to Sean, who looked like he was going to jump out of the car. I couldn't hear what she said, but I could see her lips move. He nodded, then said something in response. She laughed. Nice. At least they could stand each other.

I looked back out across the bay as we drove on. Every once in a while I'd glance back, and at one point I saw Sean and Carrie poring over his tourist attraction book. Crank and I didn't speak. The dark grey clouds rolled over us, and Crank pulled over to put the top up.

We drove on in the rain.

Just a little (Crank)

"You're turning too early," Sean said.

"Yeah, I know," I replied. "But I need to get gas, or this is going to be a very short trip." It was two o'clock in the morning and I needed to find a place to get gas, and a hotel, in that order. Julia was curled up against the passenger side door and as far as I could tell Carrie was asleep in the back seat. Neither of them had spoken in hours... Julia because she was still pissed at me and Carrie in silent sympathy with her elder sister.

So here we were, at two in the morning, headed south on I-5 in southern California, the gas gauge on empty. The sign before the exit said GAS FOOD LODGING EXIT 242, so it couldn't be far, but as I pulled off the exit, I panicked a little. Warm air blew over me, and all I could see in the darkness was sand, scrub, and flat darkness for miles. I'd stopped hours before, after the rain stopped, to put the top down.

"Shit," I muttered.

"I think you should get back on the highway," Sean said. His voice had an edge of anxiety.

"It's fine, Sean. You saw the sign, it said gas and food and stuff. We probably just need to go a little ways."

In the darkness, the night was hushed, the only sound the quiet thrum of the Mustang's engine and the wind blowing through the scrub. No other cars passed.

I could get back on the highway and hope to make it to the next exit and hope it had gas.

I could turn to the left or right on this two-lane road in what appeared to be the middle of nowhere and trust it would take me somewhere.

I could wake Julia, because she had the map, and she could tell me where the hell we were.

I sighed and closed my eyes. I turned left, because that was the general direction of Texas, and began to drive.

"I've got a bad feeling about this," Sean said.

"Relax, Sean."

And so I drove. And drove. And drove some more. The road continued, straight, between empty fields that appeared to have nothing cultivated but dust and scrub brush. And twenty-two very long minutes later, I finally saw light on the horizon ahead of us. Bright light. It had to be a gas station, or a town, or something.

I breathed a sigh of relief and sped up a little. Slowly, the light grew brighter and brighter and finally resolved itself, high above the scrub and sand—a 76 sign. I rolled into the parking lot fueled by fumes and optimism and immediately saw the problem.

The lights inside and underneath the shelter were all turned off. The station was *closed*.

I groaned. "Really?" I muttered. Maybe the pumps were still on. I turned off the car; in the dead quiet of the night I could hear the faint ticking of the engine in the heat. Julia stirred a little and I *really* didn't want to wake her up, so I got out and stepped over to the pump. It was turned off too.

I wanted to cry out, "It's not my fault!"

Instead, I opened the car and slid back in.

Julia shifted position, and in the warmest voice she'd spoken to me in three weeks said, "Hmmmmm... everything okay?"

I leaned close and whispered, "It's all good, babe. Just getting gas."

"Don't call me that," she muttered, still asleep.

"Where are you going now?" Sean asked in his usual near-megaphone.

"Shhhhh," I hissed. I cranked the car and pulled out of the gas station. "We'll just go on to the next station. One has to be open."

"I don't think..."

"Give it a rest, Sean."

It couldn't be that far to another gas station. It *couldn't*. I mean, seriously, what did the people who lived around here do? We'd just get to the next major intersection or whatever and get some gas there. I kept thinking that as hard as I could, because I was going about sixty, ten minutes later, when I felt the engine shudder. Once. Twice. Then we were coasting, near silently, running down the straight highway on nothing but momentum. The highlights dimmed slightly as the engine cut out.

I tried to think as quickly as I could. I needed to get the car off the road while it still *had* momentum, or Sean and I would be pushing. I eased the car onto the shoulder and it immediately began bumping on the loose gravel, raising a cloud of dust in the darkness. I let the car roll as far as possible, twenty, fifty, a hundred yards before it finally rolled to a natural stop.

It was quiet, nothing but darkness and stars to the horizon, a faint wind blowing through the scrub. Somewhere in the distance I heard the sound of a cricket, then another, and as the car sat there longer, the night became louder and louder with the sounds of nocturnal birds and other creatures. Did they have coyotes in California? Mountain lions? Now that I thought about it, what exactly was a coyote, anyway? I started to ask Sean, knowing that in doing so I was risking having to listen to a dissertation, but I was interrupted by Julia stirring.

"Where are we?" she slurred.

In as confident a tone as I could muster, I said, "Near Lost Hills. Just stopping to get some rest."

She murmured something under her breath that sounded suspiciously like "hotel," but I just ignored her until Sean put in his two cents.

"I think she said we should stop at a hotel."

I rolled my eyes and looked at Sean, then spoke in an urgent whisper. "Right. I'm sure she did, Sean. But there isn't much I can do about that right now."

"She's going to be mad," he observed in his normal, too-loud tone.

"Mad about what?" Carrie murmured from the back seat.

Everybody hates me.

Julia stirred again. "What's wrong?"

"Nothing's wrong," I replied.

"Except apparently you're going to be mad about something. Or maybe it's me. Unclear pronouns," Carrie said.

"I don't think it's unclear at all," Sean commented.

Julia stretched and sat up in her seat. "Where are we again?" She looked around in the darkness.

"Near Lost Hills," I said.

Carrie turned to Sean. "No, it's definitely unclear. *She* could have been Julia, or it could have been me. So which was it? Who's going to be mad?"

I rolled my eyes. "It doesn't matter," I said.

"It might," Julia said. "What the hell's going on, Crank?"

"Nothing. Absolutely nothing."

"Except," Sean supplied, "we're out of gas."

"Well, there's that," I admitted. "But it's not a big deal; there'll be a gas station somewhere."

Julia shook her head. "We're out of gas?"

"Just a little."

She groaned. "Where's the map?"

I looked around, but I didn't see it. "Umm, not sure."

Now she was wide awake. "But you know where we are, right?"

"More or less."

Julia thumped her head against the dashboard. She took a deep breath. "So... we're...somewhere. Out of gas. Not on the highway. And we don't know where exactly we are. Or the nearest gas station? Or the nearest hotel? Is that it?"

I swallowed.

Sean was helpful as always. "The nearest gas station is miles behind us, but it was closed."

Julia leaned against the door. "I'm going back to sleep. Wake me up when I'm in my bed in Boston."

CHAPTER THREE

Life in the Fast Lane

Nothing like you (Julia)

"Talk to me, sis," Carrie said.

The sun was almost up, the sky a beautiful wash of pale blues and greens. Crank and Sean were three hundred yards away and moving down the highway on foot, Crank carrying a gas can, so Carrie's question wasn't even remotely unexpected. I'd been avoiding talking about this for hours. I knew that it was coming; I knew that I was going to have to talk about it. I also knew wasn't ready. I wasn't ready to say it out loud. I wasn't ready to tell her how I felt, how much I hurt, how just fucking *awful* the summer tour had been. And the worst part of it was, neither Crank nor I had been able to talk about it.

As Crank and his brother walked away, Carrie and I sat on the hood of the car watching.

I sighed. "Okay, well. Where do I start?"

"The beginning?" Carrie was always logical.

I shook my head. "Sometimes it's hard to know where a story begins."

"Why don't you tell me about the tour then? Because last time I saw you two, you couldn't keep your hands off each other. What the hell happened this summer, Julia?"

I leaned back on the hood and stared up at the streaks of light blue now stretching across the dome of the heavens as the sun approached. I sniffled, just once. "It's been a really rough summer."

"What the fuck happened, Julia?"

I felt sick to my stomach. As if saying it out loud would make it worse. As if saying it out loud would remove any chance of fixing it.

"Spit it out, Julia! What did he do? I'll kill him if he hurt you."

I shook my head. "Not like that... It's just... Okay..." I slumped. I didn't want to talk. I didn't want to do anything but climb into bed somewhere and rest.

"Sometimes I just think we're too young to be this... serious. I don't know. I love Crank, but... Okay, back in June, we flew out to Vegas to meet Allan for the beginning of the tour."

"I remember."

I began to tell Carrie the story in halting steps as I sat on the car mostly looking away from her, playing with my hair or scanning the slowly lightening sky.

I'd never forget those first impressions when we had arrived in Vegas. For several weeks prior to our departure, I'd been working on the phone and via email with Preston Reeve, the manager for Allan Rourke's band. Preston had been helpful every step of the way, and that was a big deal, because even though I'd done a good job managing Crank's band so far, I didn't really know what I was doing. Preston had been the manager for the Rourke band for more than ten years. He knew the ropes; he knew how to deal with the venues, the hotels and the record labels. Most of all, he was a professional, and so it wasn't a big deal or a big surprise when he met us at the airport. At least not to me.

Crank, however, had been surprised. Not once during the planning of our flight to Vegas, or the planning of the tour itself, had he ever inquired about our travel arrangements, where we'd be sleeping, or what we would be doing. He had placed all of that in my hands as a matter of course, and I was okay with that. After all, it was my job as manager of the band. Apparently, he had found it alarming that the moment we walked out of the security gates at the Las Vegas airport, we were approached by Preston.

Preston was a big, bold guy. Just like me, he'd attended Harvard, though he graduated in '93, ten years before I did. He wore a blue suit coat with an open-collared white shirt and faded jeans and had a single turquoise stud in his left ear. The earring was set off by short, cropped brown hair and pale blue eyes. To anyone else, he looked cool and professional and friendly.

He approached with an easy, lopsided grin and a warm, firm handshake. "Julia? Crank? I'm Preston Reeve."

He and Crank sized each other up on the spot and I could tell neither of them liked what they saw, but we managed to get moving safely toward ground transportation. We picked up our bags and headed out to the waiting Lincoln Town Car, where Preston got into the front passenger seat and Crank and I slid into the back.

"So, Allan says you guys are fantastic," Preston said to Crank.

Crank grunted, then said, "You're one of his guys?"

I rested a hand on Crank's knee. "Preston manages the Rourke band. He's been a big help while we planned the tour."

"Oh, yeah?" Crank said, raising his eyebrows. "Preston, where you from? I can't place your accent."

"Connecticut," Preston answered smoothly. "I went to Harvard, but then headed out west... I always wanted to be in entertainment."

"Harvard, huh?" Crank said. He looked distinctly uncomfortable. "So you and Julia must have a lot to talk about. While you're being... uh...helpful."

I couldn't help it. I rolled my eyes. Crank's nostrils actually flared a little.

Preston was oblivious to Crank's mental breakdown. "A little," he replied. "Things change a lot in just ten years, but still, there's a bond between people who attended there." He gave me a warm smile. Priceless.

"Right. I was a pit rat," Crank said. "I wouldn't know nothin' about that."

"Crank," I murmured.

"That's right, you're from Boston. What clubs did you play there?"

Crank shrugged. "Metro. Bill's."

"Not the Rat?"

"Rat's closed down, has been for years. They put in a frickin' hotel."

The conversation drifted from there, not openly hostile, but not easy either. Matters stayed the same for the next couple of days. The band was busy doing final rehearsals and then on Saturday actually prepping at the stadium. The *stadium*. Because it was a sold out show—more than 35,000 seats sold at the Sam Boyd Stadium. Up until that Saturday night, the biggest show Morbid Obesity had ever played was for maybe a thousand people.

I had what seemed like a million details to attend to. Vendors. T-shirts. Roadies and the placement of equipment. Dressing rooms for the band. Someone had spilled a case of beer on an open case of dynamic mics. Thankfully, old-style dynamic mics could stand up to almost any abuse and they'd be okay, once they were cleaned and dried out... But in the meantime, I had to scramble to find an open music store to replace the mics until they were working again. I was running around like a maniac and I most definitely didn't have time to babysit Crank, who'd suddenly become a giant dick the moment Preston arrived.

I scheduled short meetings with Preston at 2 pm and again at 7 pm so we could be sure any last minute details were covered. I had to meet with him because *nothing* was going right. But Crank? He didn't like that idea at all.

At our two o'clock meeting, Preston made a useful suggestion. "You guys are used to moving around on tiny little stages in clubs," he pointed out. "And you can see it here. We've got this giant stage, and they aren't using it."

I watched the band, nodding. It was true. Right now the band was in the middle of the fourth or fifth run-through of Crank's newest song, and on this huge stage, they looked like they were all huddled together in a tiny corner.

Ten minutes later, the band had finished their set and Preston had gone on to other things. I climbed up on the stage and gathered the band. Crank was sweaty, grinning, and they all looked exhilarated. Crank and Serena fist bumped.

"Great practice!" I said.

"I'll say." Serena had an easy grin on her face.

"I've got one suggestion," I said. "Can we spread it out a little? We've got a huge stage here, let's use it."

Serena looked thoughtful and started to nod, but Crank cocked an eyebrow. "Is that Preston's suggestion?"

I blinked. "It is, but he's right. From up in the seats, it looks a little weird with the band crammed into just one section of the stage."

"I didn't know we were taking directions from the other band's manager," Crank responded.

Serena's eyebrows bunched together. "I think it's a good suggestion, Crank."

He just rolled his eyes. "Whatever. If you think we should go changing stuff at that last minute, then let's do it."

As I recounted the story for Carrie now, two months later, she grimaced. "Crank was jealous?"

I shrugged. "Yeah, I guess. He was a complete dick about it, too. And the thing was, there was nothing to be jealous of. Preston is *so* not my type. I mean he's all...preppy...and Harvard...and..."

Carrie tilted her head and raised one eyebrow. "Nothing like you at all." Then she smirked.

I sighed. "All right! So yeah, we had a lot in common. But that didn't mean Crank got to be a complete shit about it."

"What did he do?"

You Wouldn't Understand (Crank)

It had been a nice, cool summer. I thought.

As it turns out, if you're walking twenty miles through the desert with the rising sun glaring angry rays down on your neck, it feels like you opened a hot oven and walked right in. I don't think we'd gone more than a mile before I was dripping sweat and my arms were aching from carrying the gas can.

The plastic gas can. Which probably didn't weigh more than fourteen ounces.

Another thing, just for future reference. If you're going to walk twenty miles through the desert while wearing combat boots, make sure they have functioning laces. Because what looks cool on stage or walking from the car to the nightclub doesn't feel so cool when your skin starts to get rubbed raw.

I guess it wasn't really desert. Close enough, though. Sand and scrub. Dust. At first glance, it looked like the fields on either side of the road were under cultivation...at least everything grew in more or less neat rows. They don't do that in nature, do they? I didn't want to ask Sean. I mean, there's no stupid questions. But, maybe there are. Anyway. We kept walking.

It was about half an hour into our walk when Sean spoke. "Can I ask you a question?"

"Yeah, of course."

"Are you and Julia breaking up?"

"What makes you ask that?" I wanted to dismiss it. I wanted to smirk and say, "Oh, hell no, what gives you that crazy ass idea?" Instead, I felt a hole open up in my chest.

"You're always fighting with each other," he said matter-of-factly. "I don't understand why. I like Julia."

I sighed. And kept walking.

"I do too, Sean. I mean, I love her."

We walked in silence a little further, and then he said, "You should tell her that."

"It's not that simple."

"Why not?"

"Because there's stuff that happened that you don't understand, Sean."

He kicked the sand and kept walking beside me. "I see. Because: reasons."

"*What?*"

He shrugged. "That's what people always say when they don't have a rational reason for their behavior. Because: reasons. You've got reasons, but you won't talk about them. Because they don't really exist."

Irritation swept over me. "Or maybe I just don't want to talk about them, Sean. It's not really your business. She's *my* girlfriend," I reminded him.

"And she's *my* best friend," he replied.

I swallowed. And kept walking. And sighed. Sean reminding me that she was his best friend was like getting punched in the stomach. "It's all confused," I said.

"What's confused? Just be nice to each other."

I swallowed. Uncommon wisdom. But how do you get there?

"I don't know if she'll ever be nice to me again, Sean."

"Why not?"

So I told him, starting from the moment I realized she was on the phone with him three times a day for the two weeks leading up to our departure, the moment that arrogant prick Preston Reeve started hitting on Julia right in front of my eyes on the way from the airport in Vegas, the way they crowded close together during their *multiple* meetings at the stadium.

"Julia would never cheat on you."

"That's not the point," I replied. "He's a total player. She let him just...hang all over her."

The sun was fully over the horizon now, the sky a beautiful bright blue.

"Truck coming," Sean said.

Thank God.

I stepped to the side of the road. The truck was coming up behind us, a large one, and I could hear the whine of its diesel engine as it got closer and closer. I waved my arms. Even if the truck was only going part of the way to the gas station, it would be a huge help. This was taking forever. For a second, I thought the truck was going to slow down. As it got larger and larger, closer and closer, I saw a look of alarm pass across the faces of the two men in the cab. The driver had short cropped hair and blue eyes, and sneered at me. Then they accelerated, the truck tossing dust and gravel on us as it passed.

"Huh," I said.

"Why wouldn't they stop?" Sean asked.

"I thought they were going to," I responded. But then I looked down at my combat boots, spiked leather jacket and torn up t-shirt. I knew why they hadn't stopped.

My fault.

We continued on. A few minutes later, Sean spoke again. "I still don't think you make any sense about Julia. You said you know she wouldn't cheat on you. So why were you angry?"

"Jesus, Sean. Will you drop it?"

"No."

I rolled my eyes. "Because he was like a giant dick walking around in a suit. I couldn't breathe near him without smelling racquetball and polo shirts and expensive cologne. That guy...he's all fucking success and WASP and shit."

Sean raised an eyebrow. "We're so much cooler than that."

"I don't even know what that means."

"I don't know what you mean."

I shook my head. "Sean...don't you think he's more her type? I mean, he went to Harvard, for Christ's sake!"

"Did she say that?"

"No!" I scoffed. She didn't have to. "Just...Just leave it alone, all right?"

"Crank, why would I leave it alone? She's my friend. You love her. I love her. Mom and Dad love her."

"But she doesn't love me anymore, Sean."

"Why *not?*"

I shook my head. Frustrated. Angry. And from the looks of it, we still had something like eighteen miles to go. "You wouldn't understand."

"Oh yeah? Would that be because I have Asperger's, Crank? Because if it is, you can shove it up your ass."

I stopped, stunned. "What?"

"You heard me. I am so sick of you treating me like I'm broken somehow."

"Sean, you're not broken."

"Then stop talking to me like I am! I *do* understand. I understand that you're messing up my relationship with my best friend."

I exhaled, loudly. Then I started walking again. Then I replied. "She doesn't love me anymore because I hurt her, Sean. I got jealous and acted like an idiot. I broke her heart."

Sean was silent. For several minutes, the only sound was our footsteps on the gravel of the shoulder and the occasional gust of wind blowing through the scrub on either side. My mind kept turning back to that night, two weeks into the tour, when I looked up and saw her disappointed face. The night when I'd been so fucking angry with her because all she wanted to do was hang out with *Preston*. The night when she turned around and walked out without a word. The only words I could think of were *forgive me*. And I didn't say them, even though I felt them.

Apparently Sean had been mulling over my words too, because one moment I was walking and the next I was sitting on my ass beside the road, and the split second in between, I was being knocked down by Sean's fist. I didn't even see it coming. A little cloud of dust rose around me.

"What the *fuck*, Sean?"

He stood above me, pointing a finger from his shaking fist. "You hurt her? What did you *do?!*"

I was too busy holding my hand over my now bleeding nose to answer him.

"What did you do?" he repeated.

"I kissed a groupie."

Sean let out a cry. Then he kicked gravel at me.

"Fuck!" I muttered.

He stood there, shaking, looking down at me with contempt and disappointment. He kicked rocks and dust at me one more time, then turned and walked away.

I slumped. Of course there was more to the story than that. There always was. But did the *more to the story* really matter? I didn't think so.

So I scrambled to my feet and tried to catch up with my brother, who'd already moved far down the road.

CHAPTER FOUR

Where the Wild Things Are

Little Bastard (Julia)

I don't know how far they had to go to get the gas, but it took forever. Carrie and I sat on the hood of the car, and despite the fact that we were stuck in the middle of nowhere, I was as relaxed as I'd been in a very long time. Carrie and I didn't see each other often and it was great to get a chance to catch up. Whatever the circumstances.

So we spent the morning chatting. Laughing. I told her the story of Preston and Crank and our screwed up tour, and the first word out of my sister's mouth was "Fucker." Because that's what sisters are for. For the first time in two months, I felt a release of stress; a lack of pressure. I felt light and happy. I *laughed.* I'd been doing precious little laughing lately.

Sometimes you just have to laugh.

Anyway, a couple hours later, I guess, a truck pulled off the road just ahead of us, and Crank and Sean climbed out of the back. It was instantly obvious that something was wrong. Sean was stiff...well, stiffer than usual. He wouldn't look at Crank, and he walked back toward the car without a pause.

Crank came behind him. He looked tired and his nose was swollen and red like he'd been punched. My first reaction was to ask him what was wrong; I didn't like seeing him unhappy. My second reaction was to tell him to go fuck off.

I pondered my options and decided on a middle ground. I sat down in the driver's seat, without a word, while he poured the gas into the tank. Carrie got in the front seat beside me, which meant the guys could just suck it up in the back.

Crank raised an eyebrow but didn't say a word; he just climbed in the back seat and I cranked the engine and swung the car into a wide U-turn, raising a cloud of dust.

Fifteen minutes later, I pulled to a stop next to the gas pumps. "This is the station that was closed last night?" I asked.

Crank nodded. He climbed out, his back straight and angry, and pumped the gas. We all got coffee and snacks, used the restroom, and brushed our teeth, which made it a long stop, but finally, at near enough to eleven in the morning, we were on the road and on our way.

"You came from that direction?" I asked, pointing. "From the highway?"

Crank nodded. I put the car in gear and took off, staying at a careful 55 mph, unlike my maniac boyfriend who religiously stayed 25 miles above the limit.

"I've been wanting to get my hands on that sound system," Carrie said, leaning forward and turning on the stereo. She quickly scanned through the stations, finally settling on a Top 40 mix that would have Crank seething. Beyonce and Jay-Z came on the radio singing *Crazy in Love*.

"Um..." Crank winced as he spoke.

"I love this song!" Carrie shouted, a grin on her face. I winked at her and she smiled and started to shake her shoulders with the music.

"Is that really—" Crank started to say again.

I reached over and turned the radio up and started singing along.

A glance in the rearview mirror showed an irritated Crank leaning against the sidewall, clutching a pillow on top of this head. Sean ignored the music, steadily reading his book about the top tourist sites in America.

Carrie raised her arms in the air, throwing her head back and singing along. Her long neck and thin arms were exposed, her skin pale, almost white. My breath caught for just a second watching my baby sister, finally on her way to college, as a smile spread across her face.

She gave me a sly look when the song switched to 50 Cent. That was well beyond my taste too, but what the hell. I started beating my hands on the wheel as she tapped on the dashboard, and we both burst into laughter.

If I could have frozen that moment with my sister, I would have.

As it was, we just kept rolling. Two minutes later, I saw the entrance to the highway.

Crank leaned in between the front seats. "I promise to be nice. Can I drive?"

I raised an eyebrow and looked at Carrie. She shrugged. I shrugged back, then pulled the car over. Crank launched himself over the side, landing in the gravel beside the car. Carrie started to stir, but I shook my head and climbed into the back seat.

"May I?" Crank asked Carrie politely as he climbed in the driver's seat. He gestured to the stereo; I tried to stifle a smirk.

"Be my guest!" she said, grinning.

Thirty seconds later, the sounds of Natasha Atlas's *Lelsama* filled the car. Hard not to dance along with that one. And honestly I wasn't even sure what the point of all my anger and needling of Crank was. My emotions shifted suddenly from the elation I'd felt goofing off with Carrie to abrupt sadness. I loved Crank. Whenever I thought of the night I saw that kiss, I felt a gaping hole in my chest that I didn't think I had enough tears to fill. The wave of...grief—yes, it was grief—hit me so suddenly all I could do was curl up, my head on the pillow, and close my eyes.

I felt the car moving underneath me as Crank pulled out again, but I kept my eyes tightly closed. Sean was next to me in the back seat, but busy reading. Thank God. I didn't want him to talk to me right now.

I didn't want to feel this way. I didn't want to be sad anymore. I didn't want to feel this aching, dull pain in my chest every time I looked at Crank, but I didn't know how to stop it. I didn't know how to stop the tears and I didn't know how to stop the pain.

"You really should consider slowing down," Sean said. "Can I tell you something? Did you know that the Transport Research Library reports that for every kilometer per hour increase in speed, the accident risk increases three percent?"

"I know you're pissing me off," Crank replied.

"Not just that," Sean continued. "At higher speeds, injury is much more severe. When collision speed increases, the amount of kinetic energy acting on the body increases until the risk of severe injury or fatality becomes even more acute."

"What the fuck, Sean?"

"I think he's trying to say you're making him nervous by driving so fast, Crank," Carrie commented in a calm, temporizing tone.

Crank didn't answer, but I felt the Mustang slow a little. And then I felt even more confused, because it shouldn't have taken my sister saying something to get Crank to watch out for his brother. That always came naturally. Lately I felt like I didn't even know him.

Whatever. I needed to stop worrying about it. I needed to stop thinking about it.

"Um... Crank? *What is that?*" Carrie's voice was sharp, anxious, and my eyes snapped open.

"What's what?" he retorted.

Carrie didn't respond in words. Her sudden scream was piercing; terror shot down my spine. I sat up, just as Crank yelled, at the top of his lungs, "Oh, holy flying Jesus, what the fuck?"

The car swerved as Crank let out another shout and Carrie shrieked.

"Please try to maintain control of the car!" Sean shouted.

"Carrie, what's wrong?" I asked.

Her face was pale, her mouth open and eyes wide. She crammed her-self as tight against the door of the car as she could possibly go, and pointed.

My eyes followed her finger to the impossible sight of a gigantic, hairy, enormous spider crawling up the face of the center console. Crank con-tinued to scream, the car weaving all over the place. Tires screeched behind us somewhere, and then I heard the sound of a siren.

"Crank, stop the car!" I screamed.

"Really, all of this is unnecessary..." Sean said, his voice level and calm.

He was the only one calm, because Crank yanked the steering wheel over as he braked suddenly, pulling the car into a sickening skid down the emergency lane. All of us, the spider probably included, screamed at the top of our lungs as the car skidded to a stop.

Half a breath later, Carrie, Crank and I jumped over the sides out of the car only to find ourselves faced with a police car screeching to a stop behind us.

When the cop saw all of us pouring out of the car, he popped his car door open and shouted, "Everybody on the ground!"

Carrie screamed again, because the police officer, who saw all of us jumping out of the car like clowns, or gang bangers maybe, drew his weapon.

I dove to the ground. So did Crank and Carrie.

Everything went silent. Except for Sean, who was still in the car, and held the wriggling, six-inch diameter spider up in the air. He held it firmly by its thorax, and the various appendages waved and wriggled in a nightmarish display.

"I told you all, don't worry, it's not a tarantula."

The cop went pale. "What the—what? Put that thing..."

Sean smiled. "It's okay. This is a Calisoga spider. It's often mistaken for a tarantula, but his venom isn't dangerous to humans. He will bite, though."

"Sean, for God's sake," Crank said.

The cop put his pistol away. "Son, can you step out of the car and put that...spider...um...."

"Yes, sir," Sean replied.

Everyone waited in silence. Sean opened the door and got out of the car, still holding the spider in his left hand.

"Can I see that?" the police officer asked.

Crank stirred, and the cop said, "You stay right where you are."

Crank froze.

The police officer walked over to Sean. "That's some spider."

"He crawled out from under the dashboard."

"That why you all were all over the road?"

"Yes," Sean affirmed. "Plus, my brother's a terrible driver. He was speeding before, but I convinced him to slow down. Did you know the likelihood of an accident increases three percent for every additional kilometer per hour?"

"That sounds serious," the police officer agreed. "You sure this little guy ain't poisonous?" He poked a finger at the spider, who waved its legs aggressively. I shuddered.

"He isn't. But his bite will hurt."

"How do you know it's a him?"

"Educated guess," Sean replied. "You can't be one hundred percent sure. But this one, if you look here..." He pointed at the spider's...stomach?

Carrie looked up. "Can I see?"

I shuddered again.

The cop shrugged. "Come on," he said and Carrie got up, brushing dust off her front as she approached Sean and the cop.

"Right here on his abdomen," Sean continued, pointing, "you can see *apiandrous fusillade.*"

"The *what?*" the cop said.

"It's um...kind of a silk-spinning gland," Carrie supplied, which caused the cop to do a double take that she had a clue what Sean was talking about.

"Male spiders have an extra set on their abdomen. Or at least...most do," Sean explained.

"It's hard to tell without a female to compare it to," Carrie responded. "People mistake the gender of spiders all the time."

"It's true," Sean told the cop, who stared at them both incredulously. "Even experts sometimes can't tell if a spider is male or female."

I looked up and met Crank's eyes. The cop hadn't told us to get up, and I wasn't going to without permission. Crank looked over to Sean and Carrie, then back to me.

He grinned. I did too. Who else in the *world* but our siblings would have known that?

"Well," the cop said, "I guess if that little bastard had crawled up between my legs I'd have been driving all over the place too. I'm gonna let y'all go with a warning. But slow down and be careful."

CHAPTER FIVE

Magic Carpet Ride

Don't be snarky (Crank)

"Are you sure this is the right place?" I asked.

Julia was in the front passenger seat, peering at her map. She'd marked a big black circle with a Sharpie showing our destination, back a million miles and almost as many hours ago when she was planning this road trip.

She looked at the map, then back up at the gate. Her face looked frustrated and confused.

Thirty minutes before, we'd passed a billboard welcoming us to town.

SEMINOLE
Gaines County
#1 OIL PRODUCER
#1 COTTON PRODUCER
#1 PEANUT PRODUCER
#1 PEOPLE ANYWHERE

The sign was clear enough. The residents of Seminole, Texas, thought they had everything going for them. The left side of the sign even boasted a twenty-foot high number 1, extending well past the top of the billboard. Not far past the sign, we passed an old, rusted-out hulk of a 1960 Plymouth Valiant. Weeds and scrub grass grew out the rear windows of the car, which was a mottled mix of grey primer and brown rust.

The road into town was bordered on both sides by scrawny bushes, scrub grass and dirt all the way to the horizon. For a while, the only sign of human habitation was the power and telephone lines which ran from pole to pole down the left side of the increasingly narrow road. No stripes adorned the cracked and buckled pavement, and in some places soil and sand covered part of the road.

Julia stared at the gate beside the road, her face worried. Then she looked back at the map.

"This must be the wrong place," Carrie said. "Are you sure we're in America?"

Sean offered up some helpful information, as usual. "Actually, even though 85 percent of Americans live in cities or suburbs, more than 90 percent of the land area is rural. This is far more typical than Boston or San Francisco, for instance."

"I'm pretty sure this is...it," Julia said, her voice trailing off.

It was a parcel of land that looked close to the size of South Boston, scattered with undergrowth, a mountain of discarded and rotting tires covering the ground to the left of the deeply rutted gravel driveway. On the right, several abandoned vehicles sat rusting in the sun. A dirty and rusted white trailer sat almost on the horizon at the end of the long driveway.

"I guess we just go on in," Julia said doubtfully.

I shrugged and turned into the driveway. The car immediately bumped in a deep rut.

"Can I tell you something?" Sean spoke quickly. "In most states, the Castle Doctrine says that the person inside that trailer can't be prosecuted if they shoot all of us."

Carrie raised an eyebrow. "What?"

"It's true," he said. "In 1992, it even happened in Louisiana. A sixteen-year-old boy was shot and killed because he knocked on the wrong door looking for a Halloween party."

Oh, for Christ's sake. "Sean, knock it off," I reprimanded.

"Nobody's going to shoot at us," Julia assured us. "We're at the right place. I'm sure of it."

She didn't look sure at all.

"Is that true?" Carrie asked Sean.

"His name was Yoshihiro Hattori. He was a Japanese exchange student and got lost and knocked on the wrong door."

Carrie sighed sadly. "That's horrible."

"Don't worry," Sean said. "Julia's sure this is the right place."

I glanced in the rearview mirror. Carrie didn't look happy at all. The car hit another deep rut, bouncing us all in our seats and probably doing irreparable harm to my car.

"It might help if you don't drive into the deepest holes." Julia stating the obvious was clearly designed to help me stay calm.

"Thanks, sweetheart!" I replied, forcing myself to maintain a grin.

"I'm just saying..." she began.

"Don't."

She folded her arms across her chest and looked off to the horizon.

"Who exactly is it we're going to see?" Sean asked.

"Barry Lewis," Julia said.

"He was her bodyguard," I explained.

"Don't be snarky," she countered. "He was the only real parent Carrie and I had when we were in Belgium."

Of course I knew that. Julia had talked about Barry Lewis a lot, so much so that I actually felt a little envious of him. During her father's tour as a Senior Chief Muckety-muck for NATO in the early nineties, a security detail was assigned to the entire family. It seemed a little crazy, but true enough. I guess if I was that important of a guy, I'd want to make sure my family was protected, too.

I hadn't met Barry Lewis yet, but I'd never clear my mind of the vision she'd described. A lonely girl, eleven years old, with parents too busy to spend time with her, tagging along behind her Marine Corps bodyguard as he worked on his classic cars in the embassy garage. Before we met, Julia was the loneliest person in the world.

I didn't want her to be lonely any more.

At the end of the driveway, in a loose row, were five cars. All of them classics. Three on blocks, all five of them in various stages of repair and restoration. A truly ancient car, a Ford Model A, was parked a little closer to the house. The Model A was highly polished, chrome and wood paneling gleaming, the whitewall tires flawlessly clean, spokes polished and reflective.

The trailer was a large doublewide with a wood front deck decorated with potted plants. A dog barked inside as I stopped the car, and a moment later the front door opened and a beautiful German shepherd with a shiny coat of grey and brown ran out of the house, followed by a large man.

The man wore jeans and a blood red t-shirt with the USMC logo over the pocket. He was almost bald, with a very short fringe of salt and pepper hair, but he didn't look old. He had thick pistons for arms and the t-shirt was stretched by tightly bunched shoulder and chest muscles. His nose was flat against his face and slightly crooked. This guy was a warrior and knew it, but his face was round and his smile infectious. I couldn't figure out his ethnic makeup. It would be hard to find a name more Wonder Bread than Barry Lewis, but his facial features were almost Polynesian. I wasn't going to ask.

Julia's breath caught when she saw him. Then she jumped out of the car and ran up the stairs.

Lewis held his arms out and she threw hers around his neck. She didn't see it, but I did—his eyes went red and wet with tears as they embraced.

"Julia Thompson," he said quietly, his voice catching. "I never thought I'd see you again, baby girl," he admitted in a ragged, rough voice.

Jesus Christ, I thought, looking at him. First, he was massive. Frightening. Second, he was clearly completely undone by the sight of Julia as an adult.

Sean and Carrie stepped out of the car. Carrie was tentative as she watched her sister greet the man.

Lewis smiled, breaking off the embrace. "You must be little Carrie. Do you remember me?"

"A little," Carrie admitted almost shyly. "I remember you were huge, and your blue uniform. That's about it."

"Not surprised," he said. "You was pretty young last time we saw each other." He reached out and pulled her into an embrace.

Even though she barely remembered him, Carrie's face did some interesting things, her eyes watering. And then she said something in a breathy voice that nearly broke my heart. "Thanks for taking care of my big sis when she needed it."

"Oh, for Christ's sake," he said good-naturedly, "y'all are gonna make me cry. Let's get inside."

At that, the spell was broken. Julia introduced me and Sean, and the four of us, plus the German shepherd, followed Lewis inside. Just inside the door was a surprisingly spacious and well-kept living area. Two couches sat at right angles to each other, surrounding a glass-topped coffee table. The central wall was dominated by a 24x36 inch photograph of a much younger Barry Lewis in his dress blues with the three stripes of a Sergeant, holding a beautiful blonde woman in a wedding dress. He leaned back in the photo, one heel kicked out behind her, a tremendous smile on her face, their eyes meeting each other. The photo was surrounded by a mix of family photos including two little girls, both of them with dark hair and eyes.

I paused near the door as the dog began to bark again.

"Monica, *sit*."

"Your dog is named Monica?" Sean asked.

"Well, yeah. Monica Lewinsky."

Julia winced and Carrie laughed out loud.

A woman popped her head in from the kitchen. "Hi, y'all. I'm still cooking, but I'll come introduce myself in a few."

"You just get in there and cook, woman," Lewis teased.

She gave him the finger with an impish grin, then disappeared.

"Well. That's Dea, my boss."

"Your *boss?*" Julia replied.

"Well...wife...whatever," he explained and everyone chuckled. "The girls are at their grandparents for a few days before school starts again."

"That's okay," Julia said.

"It's not really. I don't understand why they insist on sending the kids back."

Watching the interaction between Barry Lewis and Julia, I realized suddenly who he reminded me of. My dad. Not because of his looks, because he looked nothing like Dad, but something in his easy smile and friendly banter. It made me feel a wave of homesickness, which was crazy, because I left home at sixteen and never wanted to look back.

"All right," Lewis said. "Dinner will be ready in forty minutes or so. Let me show you your rooms and such."

Lewis led us all down the hallway. "All right. Boys in here, girls down there."

Well, that was awkward. I couldn't even sleep with Julia? I started to open my mouth and object. Then I stopped. I wasn't going to argue with a six foot five, two hundred forty pound Marine.

Besides, it's not like we'd really been sleeping together much anyway.

Big brother (Julia)

Dea Lewis was a tiny woman, almost mousy, and even though her heels gave her an extra inch or two, in socks she was most definitely under five feet tall. Next to her giant of a husband, she looked like a midget, but she clearly didn't let her size get in the way of getting what she wanted, because as she finished preparing dinner, she began to order Barry around like she was a drill sergeant.

Like any smart man, he did as he was told.

A few minutes later, the five of us were sitting down at the table, all except Dea, who fluttered around like a bird, hauling plates, glasses and covered dishes from the kitchen to the table. She'd firmly declined offers to help, placing large white plates covered with what appeared to be balls of leaves the color of spinach in some kind of sauce in front of us.

Carrie looked interested and Sean horrified. Crank's eyes darted to me, then to Sean.

"This is lu'au," Barry said. "My favorite dish from back home."

Dea laughed. "Tacos would be a dish from home for you."

"You be quiet. Just because you raise a Samoan in Texas doesn't make him a country boy."

"What's in it?" Sean asked.

Dea smiled. "It's taro leaves, soaked and baked in coconut oil."

Crank and Sean never ate anything other than meat and potatoes. I covertly eyed both of them, but neither said a word. Sean tentatively reached out with a fork and took a microscopic bite. Then his eyes widened and he started eating.

That was proof. Sean and Crank were still basically children.

Dea smiled at Sean's zeal and finally sat down.

"You're from Samoa?" Sean asked.

"My mother is," Barry explained. "Dad's from Texas. He met her when he was in the Army, of course, and brought her back here. But we always went back home to see the family every couple years or so. Now tell me how you two met?"

I smiled. "Anti-war protest last fall," I said. "Crank's band was playing; I was part of the organizing team."

Dea frowned, but Barry said, "Good for you. So you guys met at this protest and what... started dating right away?"

I smiled and looked over at Crank, trying to hide the hole in my chest. "Not right away. I was a little slow to open up."

"Not surprised, given your bullshit childhood," he observed.

"Barry!" Dea said reprovingly.

"It's true, Dea. Julia and Carrie here, they had everything as kids. Except parents. Their parents were too busy with their own lives to be there for their kids. I was in the Corps then and had to keep my trap shut, but I can say whatever the fuck I want now."

The profanity angered his wife. She flushed red. "Not at my dinner table, you can't."

"Well..."

"Barry..."

"Sorry," he muttered. "I didn't mean to say fuck. But anyway, seriously. I loved these little girls like they was our own."

"I'll always think of you like a big brother," I said. I knew I was being a little ridiculously mushy, that was clear enough from the rolled eyeballs all around the room. I didn't care. Barry Lewis pulled me through the loneliest days of my life. I didn't have to justify my affection for him to anyone.

My eyes went to Crank. I loved him. But lately, even with Crank, I'd been feeling lonely and unsure of myself. And I didn't want to feel that way anymore.

Falling Stars (Crank)

The talk had gone on long enough, really. Don't get me wrong. I appreciated Barry Lewis on a hundred different levels, most especially for taking care of Julia when she couldn't do it herself, and when her parents weren't there for her. He was a good guy and a good friend to her. He was their family, really.

But not mine. Right now, I felt more distant from Julia than I'd felt since those cold days when she'd broken up with me after taking over as manager of the band, when we'd been all about business, all about work; when I hadn't been able to touch her or whisper in her ear or love her the way she deserved.

When Barry and Julia moved to the living room to sit and talk over coffee, I excused myself. I needed to get some air, so I stepped out into the dark Texas night and went for a walk.

Random fact I realized once my eyes adjusted: in twenty-two years of living in Boston, I'd never known that the full moon was bright enough to illuminate the ground and make it perfectly safe to walk around at night. The light was silver, unearthly, and washed over the landscape leaving deep black shadows on the blasted landscape. It was magnificent.

As I walked, I thought back over this summer and wondered why we'd so pointlessly argued. Why *I'd* responded the way I had. Because when I thought about it, there was no question, really, that it was all my fault. I'd been a jerk. I'd been jealous. Preston was a little prick, but I'd been the one to act like an idiot.

My footsteps were light as I walked, not really paying attention to my direction. The driveway was nearly a mile long, so I could just follow it and not get lost. I was probably two hundred yards from the house when I looked up and saw the sky.

I'm understating here. It's not that I saw the sky. It's that I *saw* the sky. And I took in a breath in a quick gasp, because the huge dome of the sky was speckled with thousands upon thousands of stars, so densely packed that in some places they looked like clouds.

I'd never seen a sky like that.

It wasn't silent out here, not at all... In fact, it was wicked loud. Crickets and frogs and other creatures, which I had no idea what they were, gave a loud, ongoing accompaniment to the silent symphony happening in the sky. As I stared up there, I felt peace come over me in a way I'd not felt in a long time.

And that was the moment it happened. My head was tilted back, mouth open watching the heavens, when a flash of light crossed above me in an instant, a quick line of dreams slicing across the sky. A falling star.

I quickly made a wish. Then I closed my eyes. Wishes on falling stars might be a load of bullshit, but maybe this wish, I could do something about. Yes, we'd had a rough couple of months. Yes, I'd done some stupid things. But nothing I'd said or done, nothing Julia had said or done, was unforgivable. It was time for us to talk.

I turned and began walking back up the driveway. I was probably only ten steps further when I heard the voices. I stopped immediately.

As it turns out, on a dark night in Texas, with no traffic or buildings to speak of all the way to the horizon, voices can carry a long way. It took me a long time to figure out where they were coming from, but then I finally placed it and saw two silhouettes perched on the hood of a car halfway between me and the house. The voices were unmistakable. Carrie and Sean.

It was maddening. I could *just* hear their voices, but I couldn't make out the words. Not that it was any of my business. I should make some noise and continue on my path in their direction so they couldn't mistake my approach or think I was eavesdropping. As it turned out, there was no need. Within two minutes I heard, "*God,* you are such a dick!"

At those words, Sean stood and paced. I heard a few more unclear words, then he stalked off. With Sean it's hard to tell—his posture is always stiff, his tone of voice always a little too loud—but he seemed to be angry as he walked away.

Carrie, still sitting on the hood of the car, didn't move at all. I kept walking, slowly so as to not scare her.

"Hey, Crank," she said when she saw me.

"Hey... You doing okay?"

She nodded in the darkness. "Yeah. I'm..." She shook her head, then spoke in a challenging tone. "Are all guys complete idiots, or just you and your brother?"

Huh? I slid up onto the hood of the car. It was an old seventies Mercedes with a mottled rusty hood and a cracked windshield.

I tried to look thoughtful for a few seconds. "I think it's pretty much all guys."

She snickered.

"Seriously, what's going on?"

She shrugged. "Sean ..."

I looked at her, question marks running in a small circle around my head. "Are you and Sean... um?"

"No. But... I mean...it's not..." She let out a loud growl.

I raised my eyebrows. "I don't get it."

"It's just that... I see what you and Julia have, and I'm watching you throw it all away, and it just makes me feel like you're a pack of idiots. She worships you, Crank. Do you know how rare that is? I'll be lucky if I ever find anyone I love half as much."

"What makes you say that?"

"Um, look at me. I'm fifteen feet tall. I'm a science geek. Every guy I knew in high school either froze up around me or was a complete dick. That's part of what I love about Sean."

"What do you mean?"

"Well, it's not like he's my type, but at least he doesn't constantly filter himself, afraid if he opens his mouth I'll reject him or something."

I snorted. "Sean's not capable of filtering himself."

She sneered and shook her head. "Of course he is," she retorted. "I know for a fact he hasn't told you how mad he is about what's going on with you and Julia. Which takes me back to what an idiot you are. I'd do *anything* for what you and Julia have."

I sighed. "Carrie, you know, someday you'll find a guy who will be your soulmate. Someone you would do anything for. Someone who makes you feel whole."

She gently shook her head in frustration. "When I do, I guarantee you I'll stand by him. I'll be his strength, and he'll be mine. I won't let some stupid jealous bullshit get in the way of who I love. It's a damn shame to see you and Julia doing that."

"It's not that simple," I protested.

"Bullshit. It *is* that simple. You go to her. You tell her you're sorry and ask for forgiveness. The end."

I wanted to ask why *I* was the one who needed to ask for forgiveness. She'd been a horrible, cold bitch for weeks. And that was *after* flirting with Preston Dickhead from Harvard. Why the hell didn't *she* need to apologize?

I realized thinking that way made me sound like a toddler, but I couldn't help it.

The thing is, realizing it doesn't actually change anything. I knew it was stupid. I knew I needed to go to her and ask for forgiveness. But I didn't *want* to.

I couldn't help but wonder how much that stubbornness might cost me. Possibly everything. I let out a sigh. "I don't think she'll ever forgive me, Carrie. I mean…would you?"

She leaned close and rested a hand on my shoulder. "That's something you and Julia are going to have to figure out. But don't let the chance go by, Crank. You can't let her go without trying."

I groaned and leaned back against the hood of the car, looking up at the sky. Falling stars might be bullshit, and I knew just wishing wasn't going to be enough. If I wanted her, I had to go to her.

CHAPTER SIX

Mon amie la rose

I'll talk to him (Julia)

When the sun shone through the window and my eyes opened, a thousand sweet little elves simultaneously drove roofing nails into my brain. I winced and closed my eyes and tried to reassess where I was and what I was doing.

I was at Barry Lewis's place in Seminole, Texas. I'd had a drink, or possibly two, with dinner, then more after. At one point I remember Sean and Carrie going for a walk, then Crank excusing himself. Had I talked with Barry about Crank?

I couldn't remember, which was awkward and embarrassing because I'm not a heavy drinker. Certainly not a heavy enough drinker to black out. But the last I could remember was talking in very vague terms about the tour and trying not to get into what had happened.

This was uncomfortable, in particular because I didn't want Barry beating up Crank, and there was no doubt in my mind that he would do so if sufficiently provoked.

I heard tense voices out in the hall and froze. Crank's voice. Carrie. Sean. Barry. All of them were out there, I wasn't there to keep the peace, and I might have caused the problem in the first place. I needed to get my ass out of bed and make sure Crank was okay.

I threw the sheet back and stumbled out of the bed way too suddenly, my head pounding and my body moving in a hundred directions at once. The first thing that happened was I left the bed. The second thing that happened was my head hit the bedroom door with a loud crack. I fell down to my knees, and I would have been fine from there, but apparently everyone in the hall heard my head hit the door, because a herd of feet moved down the hall like a pack of elephants on a rampage and then the door was pushed open by Carrie too quickly and too hard. The door flung open and smacked me right in the face.

"Ow!" I cried out.

"Julia!" Carrie shouted. She looked concerned. Dea, standing next to her, raised a hand to her mouth. Crank's mouth dropped open. Sean and Barry both blushed deep red and turned away, and that's when I realized that not only could I feel a nosebleed coming on, but that I also had on neither shirt nor bra.

"Shoo!" Dea commanded.

Barry and Sean immediately moved off, but Crank was stubborn.

"Julia? What—"

"Go!" Dea ordered, practically shoving him away from the door.

Carrie and Dea pushed into the room and closed the door. The two of them helped me to my feet and Carrie hurriedly wrapped me in the sheet.

"Lean your head back," Dea said, "and squeeze that nose. You've got a bleeder coming. You're a disaster, girl."

"I'm not a disaster," I grumbled. But my nose *was* bleeding.

Carrie wrung her hands. "Julia, I'm so sorry! I didn't..."

"Hush," Dea said. "She knows you didn't mean to hurt her."

I shrugged and let Dea guide me to a seat. Within a couple of minutes they had me sitting, head tilted back, a bag of ice on my nose. Which, by the way, hurt like hell.

"You want to talk about it?" Carrie asked.

"No," I replied.

"Don't do no good holding it all in," Dea said.

"What did I say last night?" I groaned as I asked the question.

"You said plenty, young lady. You said you loved him. You said you needed to stop and ask him for forgiveness."

"*What?*" She must be mistaken. She thought I'd said I needed to ask Crank for forgiveness, when actually he needed to ask for mine. "I can't have said that."

Dea raised an eyebrow and looked at me skeptically.

I sighed. "Okay. Maybe I could have said it, just a little."

She shook her head, then sat down in the chair across from me. "Julia, I'm going to give you a little unsolicited advice."

This ought to be fun.

"What kind of advice?" I asked.

"The kind that might save you a lot of heartache. The way I see it, you haven't really hurt each other yet. You've danced around it. You've played games. You've flirted with another guy, and now you know that will piss him off. Now he knows flirting with other women will piss *you* off. But am I right in saying you haven't done nothing about it?"

I shrugged. "Of course not," I said.

"He hasn't either?"

It wasn't really a question. Apparently my drunken self had covered all this territory already.

"All right, so, no harm done. Yet. But I guarantee you, if you keep this up, there will be harm. You're all mad at him, and he's all mad at you, and next thing you know, one or the other's gonna say or do something unforgivable. And I don't think you want that."

The whole time she spoke, Carrie was nodding along. Like she knew anything about love and pain and loss.

That wasn't fair. Carrie had taken care of all of us—me included—her whole life.

I sighed. "You're right."

"So what are you going to do about it?"

"I'll talk to him."

Dea gave me a no-nonsense look in the eyes and nodded shortly. "Keep that ice on there a little while longer and you should be fine. I'm gonna get back... I left breakfast going and poor Barry's liable to burn the house down."

Dea opened the door and slipped away faster than I could react, my mouth only opening as the door clicked softly closed.

You can't do that (Crank)

Julia's nose was swollen and red, but not broken. She avoided my eyes as she came to the breakfast table and didn't participate at all in the conversation, which made things impossibly awkward for the rest of us, since she was the only person at the table who knew everyone.

Carrie and Sean filled in the gap with a raucous debate about the differences between Norway rats and roof rats, which type of rat was more common in Boston versus San Francisco, and the best ways of controlling them as pests without harming the environment. And no, I am not making this up. They were like old chums bullshitting at a barber shop about baseball stats. Except they weren't talking frickin' baseball, they were talking rats and mating patterns and ecological impact and shit.

What planet were they from?

I sat there, staring at them, and at one point Barry met my eyes and grinned, raising his eyebrows. I shrugged and grinned back, then ate my bacon. Because really, what can you do?

I sat in an uneasy silence all the while they talked, feeling like the hammer was going to fall. I knew she would explode like a bomb at any minute. She looked hung over, her hair a mess, eyes bloodshot, a deep furrow in her brow where her eyebrows kept pulling in close to each other. Normally Julia was utterly beautiful, and right now she was too, but the expression on her face made me think those were fucking poisonous caterpillars walking across her face, not eyebrows. And I didn't want to get *anywhere* near her teeth, because her incisors looked deadly.

So Sean and Carrie yapped it up about... Well...now it sounded like they'd moved on to the fucking bubonic plague. Julia sat there looking miserable. I sat there feeling awkward. Dea rolled her eyes at Barry, so he got up and walked in the kitchen and came out bearing another bowl of bacon.

"Here," he said, "eat up."

"Barry," Dea warned him with her voice and her glare.

He sighed and rolled his eyes, then turned to me. "Crank, man. Let me help you out loading the car."

I blinked. Really, I didn't need any help, because all we had were a couple of duffle bags, and everyone pretty much carried their own backpacks. I didn't say anything, though, because it was obvious what he was after.

Julia saw it too, and said the first words she'd spoken during our breakfast. "Don't worry, Barry, we've got it."

He looked at her and shook his head. "We're just gonna chat." He stood up and crooked a finger at me like I was an errant child.

I kept my face blank, my posture as stoic as possible, but inside I sighed like I was a teenage girl. Julia stirred, and for a second I thought she was going to get up and defend me or something. That would have been the last straw, so I followed Barry out like I was looking forward to the conversation.

I hadn't realized just how hard the window units were working until we stepped outside into the blasting Texas summer heat. The sun hit me like a searchlight, the hot air scorching my throat and lungs like I'd stuck my head inside an oven.

Come to think of it, that might be a good comparison.

Barry looked around for a second and his hands flexed. What do you know? He didn't have any bags to load in the car.

I wasn't going to make this any easier for him.

Seriously, his whole purpose in this little talk was to basically lecture me about *my girlfriend*. To tell me I was screwing up, that I was somehow breaking her heart, etcetera. He was going to tell me he'd kill me if I ever hurt her.

Since we already had the script, it seemed like we could skip to the end where he threatened my life.

I looked down at the cinders and gravel of the driveway, then opened my mouth to preempt his attack with something sarcastic, but what came, unfiltered, out of my mouth was something entirely different than the cynical, defensive words I'd planned on saying.

"Barry, I'm losing her, and I don't know how to get her back." My voice choked up on the words *losing her*.

He clenched his fists then said what apparently came unfiltered from *his* mouth. "That's because you're a fucking child, Crank."

Well, that was more like it. I opened my mouth. Then closed it again. What he said next shook me to the core.

"She doesn't remember what she told us last night. But she wept. She wept because you two aren't talking to each other, because she let her guard down with you and now she's scared shitless. She loves you, you little prick. If she didn't, I'd have kicked your ass for hurting my little girl. As it is, you're gonna fix it if it's the last fucking thing you do."

I swallowed. "How?"

He shook his head. "You fucking talk with her, you moron! You tell her how you feel. You don't react to what *might* be a problem, you ask her about it. This fucking Preston guy... did she tell you he made her skin crawl? Did she tell you he was a complete dick and that she was lonely and needed you?"

My heart sank. "No," I admitted. "She... She spent a ton of time with him on the tour."

"Yeah, and from what she said, you went off and started behaving like a dick from day one. Like a jealous, insecure, child."

I sighed, then sank back against the Mustang. What he said was exactly right. I'd never given her a chance to talk about it, because I got pissed from day one, in the car on the way from the airport.

I failed her when she needed me the most.

"Look man," he said, "this is your only chance, because she told me—"

He cut off instantly when the front door of the trailer opened. Julia stalked out, her backpack thrown over her shoulder, followed closely by Sean and Carrie.

"That's enough talking about me, boys."

Barry met my eyes, shrugging minutely, then turned toward Julia as she approached him.

"Barry... I feel awful our visit was so weird."

He gave her a lopsided smile. "Baby girl, you've got a standing invitation. I know things are weird right now, but they'll get better."

That sentence was followed with the same death stare I was pretty sure he'd given Iraqi commandos before dispatching them. I just nodded back. I was determined not to lose her, I just didn't know what that was going to take.

We hugged and shook hands goodbye all around, and then we all started to pile in the car. She walked around to the driver's side—a very clear signal.

I handed her the keys.

She blinked, a little deflated because I think she'd been expecting a fight. Her shoulders lowered a little and she let out a breath. "You drive? I may nap a little."

"Sure," I replied.

She gave an infinitesimal smile and handed me back the keys then walked around to the passenger side.

What. The. Fuck?

Whatever. Maybe I should give in more often. We all got in the car and I cranked it up. We waved goodbye to the Lewises as we got the hell out of there.

As I finally reached the end of the driveway, I looked over at her and asked, "Top down?"

"Why are you asking me? Why don't you ask them?"

Christ on a crutch. Was all that necessary? I swallowed and looked over my shoulder. Carrie and Sean looked at me with blank faces. No help at all. I raised my eyebrows and stuck my arms out. *Well?*

"Sure, Crank, why don't you put the top down?" Carrie said.

"Awesome, thanks."

I reached for the catches on the edge of the windshield; Julia muttered something and crossed her arms over her chest. I sighed and took a breath. I mean, seriously, what had I done? What was so offensive about *asking her* whether she wanted the top down or not?

"Is everything okay?" I asked as I pressed the button and the top began folding back.

Julia rolled her eyes.

"Please," I said quietly, attempting to preserve the illusion that Sean and Carrie weren't hearing every word. Both of them had their noses buried in books they weren't reading. "Julia... I don't know what I did wrong. If you don't want the top down, it doesn't have to be down."

"What does it *matter?* I don't care if you have the top up or down. Seriously, Crank. You're going to do what you're going to do anyway. Why bother asking me what I want?"

"Oh, for Christ's sake," I muttered.

The top was down all the way and Carrie and Sean buttoned the cover down without being asked. I took a right and began driving. In a few minutes we'd be back out on the two-lane blacktop which would lead to a divided highway which would lead to the interstate and our route home. And the sooner we were moving quickly, the sooner it would be too loud in the car to hear her talk.

With that thought, I slowed down a little. Okay. It was uncomfortable. It was stressful. I felt like she was judging me and not giving me a chance, but the fact was, I'd screwed up. So I said words that were difficult for me. Sometimes really difficult. But they were necessary.

"I'm sorry."

Silence reigned in the car for the next forty-five years or so, because she didn't answer. I reached the divided highway and turned right, headed back south on US 385, a barren, empty stretch of divided highway that led over the horizon toward Odessa. I quickly got up to speed, the hot air blasting into the car not really cooling us at all. In the rearview mirror, Carrie's hair flew all over the place, and she ducked down behind the seat to try and get it tied under a bandana.

"Carrie, you want me to put the top back up?" I shouted.

She shook her head no, which was fine. But in the seat in front of her, Julia rolled her eyes.

"What?" I asked.

One eyebrow went down, the other went up, her face wearing a skeptical, mocking expression.

"Seriously? What the fuck, Julia?"

"What, you ask? Why the fuck are you so considerate now, huh? Here, you drive. Can I help you with your bags? Carrie, *I can put the top back up*." Her voice had a mocking, unpleasant tone, but the words made no sense.

"I don't get it."

Her response came at a shout. "*Of course* you don't get it, Crank! You never get it!"

"How the fuck am I supposed to get it, Julia? You aren't communicating in English! I'm sorry I don't speak sarcasm and innuendo."

"Right. So instead of talking to me, you just put your hands and mouth all over some groupie, huh? Way to communicate, dickhead."

All my resolution to slow down and stop left me. I'd planned on asking for forgiveness. I'd planned on kissing her ass until she forgave me. I'd planned on doing whatever it took. Instead, I ground my teeth and gripped the steering wheel harder as my foot pressed into the gas pedal.

"You know what, Julia? Yeah, I kissed her. Because I was *so fucking pissed*. I didn't have an emotional affair with her right in front of your eyes. You didn't hear me talking day in and day out about some girl. But I did. I heard every day about Preston fucking Reeve. Preston went to Harvard. Preston's been in the music business a decade. Preston thinks we should stand on the left. Preston thinks we should stand on the right. Preston thinks we're too close together on the stage. Preston thinks your perfect little kids will end up taking over fucking Harvard. Fucking Preston this and Preston that—are you fucking surprised I grabbed that girl's ass and kissed her neck?"

Carrie leaned forward. "If you guys are going to have a fistfight, do you think you can pull over and let me or Sean drive?"

"Why did you do it?" Julia screamed.

"To piss you off!"

My heart suddenly jumped into overdrive as I heard a loud honk. The car had drifted, at seventy miles per hour, into the other lane. Carrie screamed.

"Crank, pull the car over!" Sean yelled. "NOW!"

I'm a little bullheaded. Stupid, sometimes, even, but I didn't want to die. I hit the brakes, rapidly slowing the car, then pulled into the emergency lane.

The second the car rolled to a stop, Julia opened her door and began speed walking down the highway. I got out and followed her.

"Julia!" I called.

She kept walking. Her back was rigid, the hot breeze blowing through her hair.

"Stop and talk to me, damn it!"

At that, she turned around. Her face was streaked with tears. She came back at me in a rush, then raised a fist and hit me in the chest. Which hurt.

"You want to talk now? Why now, and not two months ago? What the hell is *wrong* with you, Crank?"

"What the fuck?" I shouted. "I didn't start this, Julia. It was you and fucking Preston."

As I shouted the words, I had to yell even louder, because a semi passed, diesel horn blaring as the eighteen wheels threw gravel and dust at our position on the shoulder.

Julia flinched, then shouted, "I love *you*, Crank! I don't give a crap about Preston! I never did. He's a creep. Why can't you see that?"

All the anger left me in a sudden rush. This wasn't some contest of my pride. This wasn't an argument with some shithead down in the pit or in a bar we were playing in. This wasn't some groupie.

This was Julia. And she was hurting.

"Julia... I'm so sorry."

"*What?*" she said, stunned at my sudden capitulation.

"I'm sorry."

"You can't do that."

I literally took a step back, winded. *What? I couldn't do what?* "I don't understand."

"Crank, you don't get to suddenly be the nice guy! You don't get to suddenly stop fighting and apologize and be reasonable. It's not fair."

I had no answer for that. I opened my mouth, then closed it.

"Say something, damn it!" Her tone was ragged.

"I was wrong," I said. "I was jealous."

"You were jealous?" she shrieked.

I sighed. And nodded. "Yeah, babe. I'm sorry. I was so fucking jealous I couldn't think straight."

Her mouth wrenched a little to the side, jaw tightening. "I was too. I've never been so angry and jealous in my life."

"I should have talked with you, not just reacted." At my words, her eyes watered even more.

"I should have reassured you," she admitted.

I looked at the ground, studying the meaningless patterns in the gravel and dust, then back up into the empty, grieving face of the love of my life. "You shouldn't have needed to reassure me, Julia. I need to trust you."

She nodded. "You do. And I need to be able to trust you, Crank."

I took a step closer to her. She reacted, instantly, stepping back, her old armor starting to settle into place, but she visibly stopped herself after a step or two and stayed in place. "I *do* trust you, Crank," she whispered. "That's why this hurt so much."

I opened my mouth to speak, and at the same time I reached out and touched her, tentatively, with one fingertip. My words came out on a breath of hope. "Forgive me?"

She swallowed, her eyes wide and tearing up, then she leaned close to me and whispered the words in my ear. "Forgive *me?*"

"I do," I replied instantly.

"I do," she said.

And then, for the first time in weeks, she was in my arms again.

CHAPTER SEVEN
The Game of Love

Not the response I expected (Crank)

It was a little bit over twelve hours from our unscheduled stop beside the road before we finally reached the banks of the Mississippi River at Memphis, Tennessee. The sun was setting behind us, casting the entire sky in shades of yellow and gold as Carrie turned the Mustang onto the Hernando de Soto Bridge.

Julia leaned against me in the back seat and together we stared up at the arches of the bridge, the spans lit up by rows of bright, twinkling lights.

For most of the last twelve hours, Julia and I huddled together in the back seat, talking and holding each other. It reminded me all too forcefully how much I missed the simple things. Running my fingers through her hair. Wrapping my arms around her. Listening to her low, earthy chuckle in response to jokes. Sean and Carrie took turns driving, taking us straight through with no stops except for gas and the occasional bathroom break.

So we caught up. We talked about the good and the bad from our summer. We talked about the tour, and our lives, and our hopes. But most of all we just touched, and reconnected. And loved.

For twelve hours straight, Sean and Carrie talked about bacteria. About ecology. Computers. Sean shouting in his loud, blaring tone, Carrie responding in her low, rich voice. It was clear she was as big a geek as my brother, and I loved that. I especially loved the fact that she was the only person I'd ever met who could stump him. The only person I'd ever met who *knew* as much as he did. Carrie loved her science. *Loved.*

By the time we were fully into Memphis, the sun was out of sight and darkness had overtaken the city. Carrie kept driving through until we reached the far side of Memphis, then pulled off the highway and followed the signs. Dixie Motor Inn. This looked...fantastic. Rustic. Seedy, really, but it would have beds.

I was wiped out, but kind of wired too, and an attached restaurant looked like it was still open. Maybe I could get Julia to go there with me so we could talk.

We parked and I followed Julia inside and she checked us in, because she'd made all the travel arrangements. I couldn't help but wonder if I should be taking a more active role in this. I mean...she was manager of the band, so she took care of that stuff on the road. But what about now? What was the right answer? I didn't know anything, except that so far I'd been doing everything wrong.

We could sort that out. This much I knew: I wasn't taking anything for granted any more.

After the desk clerk gave us keys for both rooms—we were in 210 and 212—I said, "Mind if we go talk for a bit over some coffee?"

She gave me a half-smile. "Yeah, let's do that."

So we put our bags in the rooms, me and Sean in one, Julia and Carrie in the other. I wasn't exactly happy with the arrangement, but first, letting the two seventeen-year-olds room together was a bad idea, and second, up until today Julia and I hadn't really been speaking much.

"Hey guys, me and Crank are going to go get some coffee," Julia announced after we'd sorted out the rooms.

Sean and Carrie stood there, frozen. Carrie's eyes darted to Sean, her expression unreadable, then she said, "Okay. We'll see you guys later."

That was odd. Maybe they were fighting or something. I didn't have time to deal with a couple of teenagers.

"Let's go," I said.

Julia gave them an odd look and we turned and walked along the concrete second-floor walkway. It was odd. In the car, we'd touched a lot. Constantly, really. After weeks of us not touching each other, I couldn't stop myself. Now, suddenly, I felt nervous, and the space between us as we walked toward the stairs felt like a hundred yards if it was an inch.

I wanted to touch her. I badly wanted to touch her, to hold her hand, or rest my hand on the curve at the small of her back. I loved that curve. I loved the heat of her bare skin under my fingertips, which ached for the sensation of running along the top of her jeans.

Instead, we walked downstairs. Stiff. Unyielding. Both of us suddenly more awkward than we'd been in a very long time.

The restaurant was like a downscale, ratty version of Denny's, which isn't exactly upscale in the first place. Threadbare carpet muted our footsteps as we entered the restaurant. In the background, most likely in the kitchen, I heard muffled country music.

A woman just this side of forty greeted us. "Hey there. Two?"

She led us to our seats and plopped down the menus with a smile. "Jeannie's gonna be your waitress, she'll be right with you. Can I get you started with a drink?"

"Do you have Earl Grey?" Julia asked.

"Sorry, we don't have a liquor license, but Stanley's down the road is open until two."

Julia stared at her for a long ten seconds, then shrugged. "Just hot tea, please."

"Okay, darlin'. How 'bout you?" She gave me a disapproving look. It was almost as if she thought that I—the unpleasant barbarian with spiked hair—had kidnapped the perfectly coifed Ivy League Julia.

"Coke," I replied.

She disappeared quickly.

I stared at Julia for what felt like a long time. "I fucking love you," I finally said.

Her eyes widened and her cheeks flushed. "I love you," she said.

Her voice was quieter than mine. And more cautious. I hated that caution. I hated that I was part of the cause.

"I want us to move past this."

Her response was cold and to the point. "I set out on this drive expecting to break up with you at the end."

The baldness of her statement hit me like a hammer, closing my throat up and twisting the muscles in my chest. I couldn't respond. I had no words. The longer I took to respond, the more concerned she looked. Her eyebrows slowly moved together, the furrow in her forehead that appeared in moments of anger suddenly becoming more and more prominent.

"Say something, damn it."

I opened my mouth, unable to think. "I'm paralyzed with fear," I spit out. *Where the hell did that come from?*

She opened her mouth...and just stopped. "What?" she asked, shaking her head. "What? Why?"

"Because I don't ever want to lose you and I'm afraid I've screwed it up beyond belief."

Julia closed her eyes and slowly nodded her head. "Maybe both of us need to do more listening and less reacting."

"I wish I'd done more of that when we first left on the tour."

"I do too. You know I was never even remotely attracted to Preston. He's a pompous asshole."

"That groupie I kissed smelled bad. I didn't want anything to do with her."

"Why did you kiss her and grab her ass, then?"

I looked down at the table. I had a lump in my chest, my throat swollen with shame. "I wanted you to be jealous. I wanted you to want me more than you wanted that prick."

"I didn't want him at all."

"I didn't know that. He had everything. Fucking Harvard. He's rich and connected and smart. He didn't grow up in Southie."

"He isn't you," she replied. "You're the one I want."

The waitress appeared with our drinks and we placed our order. While Julia spoke with the waitress, I studied Julia. I examined the arch of her eyebrows, her long eyelashes untouched by mascara. I scrutinized the slight flush at her cheeks and nose. I met her eyes, and when the waitress walked away, I couldn't stop myself from reaching out and taking her hand.

"I've missed you," I said.

"I have too," she whispered.

"It's not too late, is it?"

She jerked her head side to side. "It's not too late."

"What do we do to fix it?"

"What do you think?" she asked.

I squeezed her hand and said what came into my head, unfiltered by thought or consideration or anything else. "We talk. We love each other. We never stop touching each other. We never stop paying attention to each other."

She nodded, so I kept going.

"We make love. We *pay attention*."

She swallowed audibly. "What else?"

I sniffed, feeling a wave of painful emotion. "We... We forgive."

She nodded rapidly.

"Julia, I know I already asked this and you already answered it. But... Will you forgive me?"

Her eyes immediately went bloodshot and wet, almost spilling over. "Will you forgive me?" she whispered.

"Always," I replied.

"Me too."

Look. I didn't expect to say it. I didn't expect to do it. I've never been one for planning ahead. Or thinking very hard about the consequences of my actions. Or my words. So I wasn't really responsible for the next words that came out of my mouth. It was just my first reaction, my first thoughts. It was what I *really* wanted. It was me, unfiltered.

"Julia," I said suddenly, passionately. "Marry me."

She froze, her eyes suddenly wide and shocked, just like I used to look when I got called up in front of Mrs. Stevenson's eighth grade English class.

"Don't *think* about it," I urged. "Tell me what you *want*."

"Are you insane?"

I swallowed. "That's not the response I hoped for."

"You're fucking nuts, Crank. Nuts. Completely, absolutely crazy."

I took a breath, steadying myself. "Then go crazy with me."

Her eyes locked on mine, so big I couldn't see anything else, and she said the words I wanted to hear. "Yes. Yes, I will."

They're both seventeen (Julia)

"I'm not hungry anymore," I said. I couldn't take my eyes off of him. *Go crazy with me.* He'd really asked me to marry him.

I'd really said yes.

Crank smiled that same boyish, lopsided grin I fell in love with. "I'm not either."

We left money on the table for our drinks and a tip, then Crank took my hand and we walked out of the restaurant. I felt like every part of my body was alive. Alive with want, alive with need. Alive with desire. Every nerve ending in my body stood at attention, and if someone had touched me right then, I might've screamed. Just the touch of our hands as we walked side by side out of the restaurant was so intense, so warm, so beautiful... I wanted it to last forever.

We fell into step beside each other as we walked slowly down the length of the motel. It was so natural and effortless, I found it easy to forget that we'd barely done this in weeks. I couldn't decide if I wanted to hug him, hit him over the head or fuck his brains out.

His question was abrupt. "What do you say we kick Sean out of my room? Let's send them off with money to go see a movie or something."

Maybe all three.

"What do you have in mind?"

He winked and leered. "I want to show you my tattoos."

After a second, his voice dropped and he raised his hands to both sides of my face. As our eyes met, I felt my cheeks heat up. The emotional connection between us was urgent and intense.

"Jesus, Julia. I want to hug you forever. I want to hold you in my arms all night long. I want to make love to you. But more than that... I want to touch you. I want you to be mine."

I put my arms over his shoulders, pulling him in closer as his hands moved to my waist.

"If you want me to be yours, you might just have to *make* me yours, buddy."

Crank just grinned, then ran his teeth along the right side of my neck. I felt goosebumps rise to the surface of my already too sensitive skin.

"Let's go," he growled and broke away, grabbing my left hand and pulling me along behind him.

I felt a tense excitement, familiar and strange at the same time. My breath was shortened, my skin literally tingling.

"I'll talk to Sean," he said.

"I'll talk to Carrie."

Fifteen seconds later we got to our doors and then the damnedest thing happened. Crank opened the door to his and Sean's room, no problem. Mine wouldn't open. I tried it again, sliding the key card into the slot. The light turned green, the door clicked, the knob turned, but the door wouldn't open.

"Something wrong?" he asked.

I shrugged. "It lights up green. I think the deadbolt is on."

"Huh. Sean?" he called into his room. He stepped inside, and I heard him call Sean's name again.

A moment later he came out, looking confused. "I don't know where he could have—"

I tilted my head, looking Crank in the eye. He saw my look and stopped talking. I darted my eyes toward the other room.

"No," he said. "Sean's seventeen."

I raised my eyebrows.

"No…" he repeated. "Not like I was… Besides… Him and Carrie?" He looked confused. Baffled. *Idiotic.*

"They're both seventeen. And they bond over spiders and fruit flies and I don't know what all else."

Crank literally staggered. "Dad will kill me."

"He will not. Jack would just chuckle and give Sean a high five. What's wrong?"

"He's still a *kid.*"

I sighed. I took Crank with one arm and knocked hard on my door with the other. "Crank. Shut up. He's not. Carrie's not a kid either."

"Then… Why are you knocking on the door?"

I rolled my eyes. A second later, the door cracked a little. The latch was still engaged, preventing it from being opened all the way. Carrie's eyes peered out at me.

"What do you want?" she whispered urgently.

"Do you have birth control?"

"*Oh, for Christ's sake!*" she cried, then slammed the door in my face.

I shrugged. "I've done my duty."

Crank assessed the situation, then made the correct decision. He took me by the arm and pulled me into the other room, letting the door shut behind us.

Darkness descended instantly and I began shaking. Hard. I'd promised to forgive. I'd asked for forgiveness. It felt like having a bucket of ice thrown on me. A chill went up my body, goosebumps forming on my arms. We'd been fighting so much, it had been almost three weeks. Three weeks since we'd touched each other. Three weeks since we'd made love. And almost two months of hurt feelings, of anger and miscommunication.

For just a second, I felt my old mask of chill reserve slip back over me. My mask of pain and ice. The mask which had protected me for years, but then almost destroyed me.

Crank put his arms around me and I cringed for just a second. Crank had hurt me. He'd gotten jealous and kissed some groupie and grabbed her ass, and next time he might do worse.

"Let go, baby," he crooned in my ear. "I won't hurt you."

I squeezed my eyes shut, hard, then I felt it, the reserve and armor swept away by the low rumble of his voice. He swept his left arm behind me and under my knees, then lifted me off my feet and carried me to the bed.

My breath caught, then picked up again, noticeably faster and tighter. I felt my pulse at my throat and in my chest. He lowered me to the bed with the care and precision of a surgeon. A faint light shone through the window in a single vertical line that ran the length of his body where he stood over me.

My breath began to speed again as he unfastened his buttons one by one, slowly uncovering his tanned, muscular skin. Involuntarily, I felt the muscles in my back tighten, arching my back, pressing my breasts against my shirt.

"What..." I said. My breath came in and out too quickly to make any sense.

His lips curled up in a crooked grin. Nude now, his erection unashamedly at attention, he leaned toward me and began to peel my t-shirt off. The touch of his fingers against my bare skin caused me to convulse a little.

"What..." I said again.

"I'm going to make love to you now, Julia Thompson." As he spoke, his eyes looked into mine. Open, exposed, vulnerable.

I know I'm usually in control. But now I'd lost any control. Crank tugged at the button of my jeans, unzipping them, and pulled them and my panties off in a single, swift motion. I closed my eyes as he moved closer.

I gasped and jerked as his lips touched the ridge of my hip bone on my right side and both of his hands clamped firmly on my waist. I let out a slow cry as he trailed his lips along my stomach, then nipped at the underside of my ribcage.

I leaned my head up to kiss him, but he just smiled and shook his head, then kissed my chest just between my breasts. I wanted to tell him *stop*, to move it along, but then his hand touched me on the stomach and began moving in lazy circles, closer and closer.

It was excruciating. Every time his hand moved close to me, my hips arched involuntarily. I breathed faster and faster as his lips touched my collarbone. My neck. And then one finger, and another, were inside me, and my world narrowed in like tunnel vision, everything wrapped around the feeling as he slowly spread me open with his fingers, then slipped them deeper and curled them up toward him.

My muscles tightened around him as he slid his fingers in and out. Slowly. Then faster and faster until I began to shudder. I'd lost awareness of all my surroundings, everything fading in a haze of sensation and touch and love. One wave after another crashed over me and my voice rose higher and higher.

When he slowed down, I twisted and protested. "Don't stop!"

His lips were next to my ear. His hot breath. "Tell me you love me, Julia. Tell me you want me."

I sucked in a breath, unable to control myself, and whispered, "I love you, Crank. I want you so badly."

His fingers slipped out, leaving me suddenly cold, and his eyes bore into me. "I love you, Julia. No one else. I'm yours."

The next few seconds were so intimate they were excruciating. And then he plunged into me.

His eyelids fluttered and my neck arched back, begging him to kiss it, to bite it, to do whatever he wanted. What *I* wanted was for him to move fast and hard. But he went slowly, very slowly, gazing into my eyes.

"Faster," I demanded.

He shook his head. "I want this to last forever."

I let out a moan at his words. His hips tensed as he slowly pushed in. My body gripped around his, legs wrapped around his ass. I fought for a grip at his back, my nails digging in, hut he refused to move faster.

Slow. So excruciatingly slowly, he moved in. And back out.

I let out a loud cry as he slid back away, then in again, a little faster this time, but still teasing, still driving me to the edge of insanity. He stopped as he was almost all the way out and lowered his mouth to my breast, teasing, his tongue circling my nipple, barely touching.

I let out an involuntary growl, clutching his back. "Harder. Now." My voice was fierce, demanding, and Crank responded, lowering one arm to push my leg back hard against my chest. Suddenly he was moving as fast and hard as I'd demanded, his breath growing loud and hoarse.

Even as Crank's lips locked on mine, our tongues working together furiously, he began to move in and out, hard and fast, the slapping against my thighs forcing my legs back wider, straining every muscle in my body.

I pressed against him, my hips moving back and forth, my fingers raking down the skin of his back. I wanted him *closer*. His breath was hot and wet against my neck, one arm hooked around my leg, the other planted on the bed, bent at the elbow and wrapped behind my head.

"Julia, I fucking love you." His voice was full of need. His hips, narrow, muscular, pounded in to me, harder and harder, driving into me like a piston, and I felt waves of layered sensation moving up my body.

Even then he didn't stop, didn't let up, and his voice just grew louder and louder, and I found myself crying out, calling his name, screaming, "Crank, I love you!" as loud as I could until we both collapsed, spent and exhausted.

CHAPTER EIGHT

The Road I'm On

I could live here (Crank)

thick, warm breeze blew off the Potomac River and past the monuments. It was late, well past midnight, and the Mustang was parked on 17th Street in the shadow of the Washington Monument. The monument was lit up, brilliantly white, towering over the four of us as we sat in the grass.

"It was only a couple hundred feet from here that we met," Julia said, looking at me with a smile.

"I love this city," I replied, grinning back at her.

Carrie was standing a few feet away from us, staring at the Washington Monument. Sean lay on the ground.

"Are we done?" Sean asked.

"I could live here," Carrie said. "I always loved DC."

Julia shuddered a little. "I love that me and Crank met here on the Mall, but before that, I don't have any memories of this city."

Carrie nodded, then shrugged a little. "Maybe make some happy memories. This seems like a place I could do that."

I could see it. She was so smart and confident. Like Julia, but about different things. Despite her consistent denial of any resemblance, Julia had so obviously inherited her father's gift for negotiation and business. Carrie, though… Her personality and talents were very different. She seemed to be driven by an insatiable thirst for knowledge I'd never seen matched by anyone but Sean.

"Why not San Francisco? Or New York?"

Carrie shrugged. "New York I could see. I can't wait to start school. But I don't want to live near Mom and Dad. I mean, I love them and all, but I'm so tired of Mom being all in my business."

"Your mom loves you," Sean said.

Julia sat up straight, shocked. So did I. Sean had spent all of twenty minutes around Julia and Carrie's mother, and not under ideal circumstances. How would Mr. Analytical have formed such an opinion in such a short amount of time?

"I'm sure she does," Carrie said, "but that doesn't make her any easier to live with."

"I think she has secrets," Sean replied.

Carrie tilted her head. "What makes you say that?"

"I don't know." Sean went back to looking at the stars.

"Come *on*, Sean," Carrie needled. "There has to be something behind what you said. Some evidence? Anything?"

He sat up. "They never touched each other. Or even looked at each other."

"*Who?*" Carrie replied.

"Your parents."

Carrie and Julia looked at each other and I could see the wheels turning in Julia's brain. But we didn't talk about it anymore.

You can't be too careful about radiators (Julia)

You can always tell New York City in the summertime by the distinctive smell. Was it the subways? The shallows and wetlands of New Jersey? Was it the massive landfills, or Staten Island, or the garbage waiting to be collected? Whatever it was, every time I visited New York in the summertime I wanted to turn around and drive away.

Today, though, I didn't have that option. We entered the city through the Lincoln Tunnel, then drove north toward the Columbia University campus. Along the way, I thought the smell might dissipate as we neared Central Park or the campus, but no luck.

It was close to four in the afternoon by the time we finally found parking, located the housing office, got Carrie's keys, and moved her into her new room. It was a tiny dorm room with cinderblock walls and scuffed tile floors with a small bookshelf built into the wall below the window. Two twin beds occupied nearly half the available floor space.

Once we got her bags upstairs, Carrie practically bounced on the bed.

"I can't believe it!" she cried.

"It's kind of a crappy room," Sean pointed out.

"I know, but it's *mine.*"

"And your roommate's," he replied.

"Who cares?" Carrie replied. "I'm so excited!"

I sat down on the bed opposite her. Whoever her roommate was going to be, she hadn't moved in yet. The bed was bare and shelves unoccupied.

"What does your week look like?" Crank asked.

"Orientation on Monday," she said. "I need to get my work study assignment."

"You too?" I asked.

"What?" Crank said. "Aren't your parents paying your tuition?"

"Even though Dad donated like a million dollars or something to the school, he still makes us apply for work study," Carrie explained. "I think he paid so they'd have a position for us."

Crank looked confused. "He did the same with me, Crank. I kind of get it... If you had kids, you'd want them to have to work for something, wouldn't you?"

"Yeah," he replied. "Good point."

Sean looked intently at the radiator. He leaned close to it, as if study-ing it, then pronounced, "The odds of your radiator exploding or caus-ing severe injury are limited. This system looks well-maintained."

Carrie burst out laughing, but her eyes also went a little watery and red. "I'm sure I'll be okay, Sean."

He turned away from the radiator, looking annoyed. "You can't be too careful about radiators."

She sniffed. "I'll miss you. It's been a lot of fun during the drive."

"I'll miss you, Carrie," he said.

Sean's eyes watered, and that got me going too. Next thing I knew, the four of us were all hugging and slobbering.

"I don't want you to go," Carrie whispered into my hair.

I leaned my head against hers. "You'll be all right. You're the stron-gest woman I know."

She shrugged. "Of course I am. But I'll still miss you guys."

"Can we come visit?" Sean asked.

"I'd like that," Carrie replied. "Please do. You're my friend."

"How about next weekend?" Sean suggested.

"Might be a little longer than that, Sean," Crank said. "Give her a chance to get settled in. And you too. I think you're gonna be pretty busy once you start school too."

With a lot more tears and hugs and kisses, the three of us left Carrie behind. Crank drove with the top down. Sean slouched down really low in his seat, forcefully turning the pages of his book and ignoring every-thing, which is what he always did when he found something emotion-ally overwhelming.

I looked back and waved at Carrie, who stood in the doorway of the building, a bittersweet smile on her face as we drove away. She was so sad to say goodbye, but at the same time, so excited. I was excited for her. She was stepping into a whole new reality, away from our parents, away from everyone, really. Who knew what might happen? She might become a famous scientist, or fall in love, or run for President, or any number of things.

One thing I knew for sure. My sister was strong enough for whatever would come her way. As Crank pulled into traffic and we drove away from her, I watched her waving in the rearview mirror and hoped the future would be kind.

When Carrie was out of sight, Crank gave me a smile. "You'll miss her, won't you?"

I nodded and sniffed. "I remember how lonely I was my first year of college."

He reached out and took my hand. "She'll be okay. She's got you as a big sister."

I squeezed his hand back and wondered how I had ever gotten so mad I'd thought about leaving him.

"I love you, Crank."

"I love you, Julia."

The End

www.ingramcontent.com/pod-product-compliance
Lightning Source LLC
Chambersburg PA
CBHW020549130626
46552CB00007B/2816